April 2004

For Len and Bev —

Karpstein Was Hiding

We are so
Lucky to
have you
as neighbors!

Warmly,

Martin

Karpstein Was Hiding

Pieces of a Life

Martin A. David

Writers Club Press
San Jose New York Lincoln Shanghai

Karpstein Was Hiding
Pieces of a Life

Published by Writers Club Press
an imprint of iUniverse.com, Inc.

Karpstein Was Hiding is a work of fiction. The names, characters, places and situations described in the book are either products of the author's imagination or are used fictionally. Any resemblance to actual events, locales or to persons, living or dead, is coincidental.

For information address:
iUniverse.com, Inc.
620 North 48th Street
Suite 201
Lincoln, NE 68504-3467
www.iuniverse.com

ISBN: 0-595-09520-8

Printed in the United States of America

Dedication

Karpstein had two mothers: The character's mother who appears sporadically in the pages of the book and the mother of the book itself.

This book is dedicated to my beloved wife, Sarah, who nursed the book along through every stage, as my devoted partner, my encouraging cheerleader and my insightful editor. Thank you, Sarah, for believing and for being.

When his own footprint and its echo become "the enemy" haunting him—when his own mind becomes the stage on which the drama rehearses. Where will he go, this wandering Jew?

What are you hiding from?
Why do you ask?
Who are your hunters?
Who have they always been?
Why won't you answer?
Am I not responding?

Survivor without a tattoo

I survived the camps at Buchenwald at Bergen-Belsen and far worse.
But no obscene numbers stain my aging arm.
The stench of carnage still burns the nostrils of my mind.
Yet the mud blood earth clings to no shoes or clothes or part of me.
I was not there.
But I survived.
I am a Jew of "a certain age;" born in a time when monsters stalked.
My young eyes looked, from the comfort of an untouched land,
For my parents faces—-and my own—-
In those firewood piles of corpses the newsreel cameras showed.
The distant cousins, great aunts and uncles (all up in smoke) my
      bubbeh wept for bring my tears too.
"Survivor guilt," my therapist said, as I cried and cried.
I was not there.
But I survived.
Endured the amputation of roots, wounding of my culture, death of
      my *shtetl*.
You who were there, your nightmares are not mine.
I have nightmares of my own.
My horrors do not match your horrors.
My memories do not run and hide from me like yours.
I am a survivor without a tattoo;
Scared and scarred in other ways.

Acknowledgements

My thanks to all those who read the manuscript in its various forms and gave comments and encouragements. Thanks to my teachers and to all the writers, the ones I know personally and the ones I have read. You gave me a love of language.

☙ I

Karpstein waited until the delivery truck was nothing more than a hollow, distant clatter. He took a deep breath and listened for the sound of marching feet. He heard none. There were no patrols. He made his move.

He rolled out of his hiding place, a sloping depression the size of a basement window. It had once been a coal chute. He came to his feet in a crouch and ran, like some strange, scuttling, hunched up creature, until he was hidden behind a garbage can. Another short pause to survey the area for dangers and then he sprinted the rest of the way down the alley.

A small flatbed farm truck had just made its weekly pre-dawn rounds and Karpstein's target was a stack of wooden boxes just delivered outside the back door of a local produce store. He worked fast, twisting the wire that held the box closed and prying up one corner. Apples. He took five from the corner of the box and then shook the box to make the others fill in the space. Then he twisted the wire to close the box again. They must never find out or they'd hunt him down. He dropped the apples into a dirty burlap bag he carried and performed the same opening and harvesting operation on a box of broccoli. He took small pieces that had fallen off the main stalks. Raw broccoli made him ache with gas, but it was food. Karpstein reached through slats on some boxes and pried others open until some cabbage leaves, six oranges, four unripe bananas and a small head of lettuce followed the other prizes into the sack. Karpstein was careful to never take enough to arouse suspicion.

The bakery truck had rumbled past just before the farm truck and if he were quick enough he could add a few fresh rolls to his food stock.

Footsteps and voices on the street. Karpstein froze and listened. It was not a patrol, but he still had to be careful. Even innocent civilians would turn him in if they saw him. He never read newspapers, but he was sure there was a tempting "Jew bounty" being offered. He crouch-ran to a garbage can and hid behind it until the two early morning walkers passed. Then he retreated up the alley. No rolls today, too much danger.

End-of-night gray was just giving way to smudges of pink when Karpstein's prowl-run through a maze of alleys and seldom used passageways brought him to the final obstacle in his dash for the safety of home. In an alcove in a trash-strewn courtyard a round, textured cast iron disk was Theodore Karpstein's front door. He looked to make sure the small popsicle stick he had wedged in the crack around the cover hadn't been disturbed. He was too clever to walk into a trap. A small stick jammed between the cover and the metal rim would, with its absence, serve as his warning signal if someone else discovered his secret doorway.

Karpstein had ascertained, through a strange choreography of scuttles mixed with sudden stops and 360 degree scanning turns, that he hadn't been followed. The last stretch of this part of the route was through the basement of an old school building with a loose window latch. He planned that segment of the secret sneak run journey so even if they had planted rooftop cameras there was no way they could have seen him. At the other end of the school's damp cellar a broken door let him out to a locked-in alleyway that had once been a street.

The faint light, part leftover electric glare from the quickly fading nighttime and partly the blush of morning sky awakening, revealed the thin, sallow Karpstein half squatting, half kneeling on the street outside the old school with his fingers in two round holes in a manhole cover. He was struggling to lift it. The cover was small but heavy. Karpstein had been much stronger, a trained boxer, but life in exile had taken its toll. He finally got it moved with a surge of effort and the exertion made him fart. Karpstein turned his head as if to say "excuse me" to anyone who might have heard. He had lived in total isolation for more than a year, but some habits wither slowly even outside the sunlight of society.

When the cover was moved, Karpstein hitched the sack to his belt and climbed into the dark hole. A metal ladder fastened to the slightly damp wall led into the cavern. Karpstein climbed far enough down to reach up and lower the lid on his entrance again. Twenty rungs to the bottom with the only light a faint glimmer through the finger holes in the manhole cover. Then a crouching, crawling walk through a smelly, brick tunnel with a metal pipe-lined ceiling. One hundred and eight groping steps to a metal door with rusty spring hinges. The shrill squeak of the hatch being pushed open set Karpstein's nerves on edge. He always cringed, waiting for some indication that others had heard the noise. No sounds other than a slow drip of water somewhere and the distant, occasional clank of pipes came to him.

The noisy door opened into a long, narrow grotto filled with the eerie glow of daylight filtering through a series of gratings far above his head. Karpstein's stomach clenched and he felt his mouth grow dry. He could walk upright on this part of the journey, but it was a passage of terror. This was where he was often confronted by Herman and his pack. More than once he had been so frightened by their menacing advances that he had dropped his food sack and run for his life. Better, he reasoned, to go hungry for a few days than to die in an underground battle with a swarm of hungry rats. The largest was a particularly ugly creature with a crooked front fang that gave him a perpetual snarl. Karpstein had read somewhere that facing one's fears and naming them would lessen their impact. He called the rat leader Herman, but the terror didn't diminish even a little bit.

A lone rat scampered along a pipe above his head. Another raced for a hole in the wall, as afraid of Karpstein as Karpstein was of him. Two hundred and eighty steps, right turn, two hundred more and then another spring hinged hatchway—this one far less strident in its squeaky complaints than the first. Seldom any rats past this point. Through the door and into a circular black chamber forty steps across.

The walls, for as high as the eyes could scan in the dim light of occasional rust holes and ventilation grills, were ringed with neat rows of rounded rivet heads. A large hole 20 feet from the bottom, an intake vent, led to an octopus of ducts inside the building. A skinny metal ladder, reaching into the darkness, was fixed to one side of the huge tube.

Karpstein climbed. He did not let the random slippery rung that tried to disrupt his footing or the unexpected sharp flake of rust that bit his hands distract him. He didn't think of the height. Three hundred and six rungs to the top. The massive tube had once served as a heat exhaust shaft for huge steam boilers.

Near the top a crawlable pipe just four times the length of his body angled off from the main part of the cylinder and led him home. Home was two compartments of a dusty, dead end attic in an old building, which now served as a warehouse for long-forgotten household goods.

The only other entrance to his private chambers was a trapdoor with a drop ladder that led to a hallway. Karpstein's fear of discovery made him block the trapdoor so thoroughly that it could be opened only from the inside. A ladder that folded down when the trapdoor was opened lay useless on top of the square door, its joints wedged inactive with a length of 2x4 and held shut with a piece of rope.

The building had gone through many transformations. It had been a charity hospital, a military prison hospital, and then a psychiatric hospital at a time when that phrase meant storehouse. After that, with its stench not thoroughly cleaned away but only lightly covered, the building became a county-run general hospital. The tall stack up which Karpstein climbed to enter his hidden rooms had, in each of the incarnations, been the heat exhaust for the boilers of the hospital laundry.

Over the years the succeeding administrations had built new wings, new sections, and even added new floors. The compound grew with no overall plan but rather with the opportunism of a weedy shrub. Where there was space, or where a slum could be torn down to make a space, the hospital grew. As a result there were rooms, tunnels, stairways, chambers, compartments and cubbyholes piled upon each other and intertwining beyond the capability of any set of plans on paper to define them. Karpstein knew the lifelines and arcades, the corridors and passageways of the architectural monstrosity better than its contemporary occupants, but no one living knew it all.

When a new hospital was built in the city, the old structure stood empty for more than a year and then became a factory. In the days when the building had echoed with the commotion of manufacturing Karpstein spent about a year working there. In those days his attic space had been the living quarters for a custodian/janitor. The branch of pipe through which Karpstein entered the rooms had provided that previous resident with a small amount of heat—and probably bad smells—wafted up from the machinery ten floors below. The former tenant used only the trapdoor and folding stairway as an entrance.

A small sink in one corner provided Karpstein with a trickle of brackish water. A somewhat working toilet stood in a windowless space the size of a broom closet. Karpstein had found a small card table and a ragged mattress in his hiding place. The rest of the furnishings consisted of some small wooden boxes and an old red chair the current tenant had dragged in. The boxes served as shelves for an odd assortment of kitchen utensils, a plastic tub that held the day's water supply, and a handful of scavenged plates and bowls. Several bedraggled blankets and a few odds and ends of clothing, all gathered in his wanderings, lay, folded, in two stacks in a corner. A collection of well-worn books was arranged in a row near the mattress. A tattered calendar hung on one wall. It was a Jewish calendar with lunar-based months listed by their Hebrew names. A light-stingy bare bulb dangled above each of the two rooms of the kingdom. Karpstein lived simply.

Some years before, while he worked as a shipping clerk in the then thriving factory Karpstein had found this hideout. Karpstein explored wherever he was. He knew of dust-filled closets and forgotten basement rooms in every house he'd ever lived in and in every building where he had worked. He knew the tunnels and attics of this building better than most and when he decided it was time to run, he ran here.

∽ II

"Run, Karpstein, run home to yer mamma, you little Jew bastard."

"Run Jewboy Christ-killer."

A rock flew past just an arm's length away from his head and clattered ahead of him on the street. He outran it. Home to his mother, that was exactly what he had in mind. Breath bubbled in his chest. His face hurt. Blood from his nose ran into his mouth. Salty.

"Salty blood… Run home… Is it kosher? Run home… Keep running. They're not following… Maybe they are… Next time don't take the shortcut… Run home… Blood in mouth…not kosher."

Karpstein tried to spit out the blood the trickled from his nose into his mouth while he ran and chanted. He started to cough. The bubbles in his chest grew and began to hurt.

"Keep running...run home...don't get asthma...don't get asthma...please God...If I don't get an asthma attack I'll memorize a whole page of Talmud."

A gang of neighborhood toughs waited near the Hebrew school every once in a while and waylaid stragglers who dared to wander through vacant lot weed jungles. Public school had let out two hours before and the students from Rabbi Machlis' afternoon bar mitzvah class, wearing yarmulkes and carrying books when the rest of the neighborhood boys were wearing baseball caps and carrying playthings, were easy to spot. Some of them fought back, but Karpstein just bled and ran. This was his third skirmish with the bullies. Once they had broken his glasses and another time he wore purple bruises across one side of his ribcage for a week. This time they didn't catch him by surprise and he managed to run away, but not before a rain of punches had bloodied his nose and a pair of dirty hands had torn his shirt.

"Run away...run home...run...run...run run...run run... Rambam...run run...next time don't take shortcut."

He was gasping. He felt waves of nausea fighting to take command of his stomach. He knew his mother would scream and weep and wash him as if he were a baby instead of a 12 year old who was almost a man. His father would just scream. It would be a scream of rage at the assailants and at the injustice and at injustice in general, but the numbed target receiving the overflow of verbal abuse would be young Karpstein.

Karpstein, now, more than 40 years later, still kept his knack for knowing when it was time to run away.

∞ *III*

Karpstein coughed. The dust in his hiding place did constant battle with his weak lungs. He spit.

"This lousy dust will kill me. If I get a cough someone is sure to hear me and turn me in."

Karpstein became a silent ghost in his garret during the day, but he dared not venture out. At night his freedom expanded. Karpstein's fears grew and waned like the phases of some private moon. This night his fear told him it was too early for him to flush the toilet, but he used it anyway. He half sat and half squatted on the lopsided, seatless bowl.

If he pulled the plunger the watchman might hear. The rusty pipes sometimes moaned like torture victims and sometimes sang like spirits from some mysterious netherworld. Alone in his hidden cell Karpstein often imagined he heard answering voices howling from somewhere deep inside the building. On other nights he let the building sing and added his own careless, unheeded notes. During the day the general noise of work from the building and the neighborhood masked any sounds he might make.

The daytime brought to him, via pipes and airshafts, a cacophony of telephone rings, of voices, of rolling furniture dollies, of elevators, of downstairs toilet flushes, of door slams, and of traffic on seldom traveled surrounding streets. At night the other players went home and traffic faded. Then, when he wasn't on forays after food, Karpstein and his building played a hushed symphony of their own invention.

When darkness came the warehouse workers, with the exception of the complacent and lazy watchman whose rounds were better measured by calendars than clocks, went home. Karpstein, the building's night-time master, soemtimes stayed in his room and read, but sometimes prowled the streets outside his palace in search of food. Often he roamed the warehouse's inner spaces. He was like a borer beetle tunneling through a rotted log as he moved through the edifice. He knew crawlspaces connecting to chambers linked with corridors which led to unused stairways. Ventilators, catwalks and shaky ladders were all channels of exploration for Karpstein.

But now it was day. The others had again taken over Karpstein's building. Far below a safety gate clanged shut and somewhere above him a motor whined. Freight elevator—a familiar sound. The walls vibrated as the elevator hummed upward. It crunched to a stop about two floors below him. Gates opened. Sounds of a dolly, too light to have anything on it but still squeaking like some yapping dog, being pulled along the corridor. Karpstein had heard the sound before. It meant something was being taken out of a storage space. Some trunk or dresser or something was being taken out of its cell, away from its friends the davenports, secretaries, breakfronts, sideboards, divans, boxes of dishes, lovingly packed books and photo albums and all the other echoes of lives put on hold. For Karpstein knowing that a stored object was being redeemed was as amazing as it might be for the spectral inhabitants of a graveyard to see one of their own taken suddenly back to the world of the living. He felt himself surrounded by death, or at least by its signs and souvenirs. The caged and boxed belongings in the thousand cells and spaces around him were the residue left behind by rolling stones who couldn't gather it; the effluvia deposited by swirling flows of travelers who would never return; the sudden precipitation from households dissolved by divorce or death do us part. It was, in some cases, the remaining goods the pawnshop wouldn't accept but still too good, or sentimentally endowed, to throw away.

These dead inhabitants normally were carted away, a room at a time, at least a-year-and-a-day after the rental fee checks stopped coming in. They were taken to mount the slave block and be bid on by merchants, broke young couples who were furnishing apartments and the general looky-loo assortment of curiosity seeker auction goers. When that day was at hand, about 4 times so far during Karpstein's eleven months of residence, the sound was that of a stampede as a crew roamed the halls picking out the expired rental lots for disbursement. New arrivals also sounded different.

The sound from below, Karpstein noted with interest, was a singular departure. Perhaps outside, in that other world Karpstein had escaped, one owner still cared and some remembered, comforting chair, had been ransomed. Karpstein saw himself as just one other chair serving a sentence in this mansion of abandonment and wondered how his own term would end. Would he also be redeemed or found and tossed down the airshaft into the pile of things deemed too wretched for auction?

Karpstein looked at himself in a cracked mirror he kept in his room. He thought the face looked very gentle. Sometimes he didn't fully recognize himself and he had to look hard to make sure. The face changed all the time. There was even more gray in his beard. His hair was getting long again. Karpstein kept an old pair of scissors and a grooved, flat stone. He wet the stone slightly and ran the scissors at an angle over the stone. An old man in the factory had shown him how to sharpen a pair of scissors. Karpstein was not good at the job and his scissors always tugged at his hair when he cut it. But they did cut—his hair and his greying beard. Karpstein made sure to trim his hair and beard even though hardly anyone ever saw him. He was careful not to let himself look like what he was—a frightened hermit hiding in the isolation of his own fear.

IV

Airshaft. There was an airshaft in Karpstein's hidden place.

In the building where Karpstein lived as a child, good kids didn't play in the airshaft. Rats in the airshaft. Danger in the airshaft. Rotting muck in the airshaft.

Shirley Biagelli from Karpstein's second grade class got bitten by a rat while playing in the airshaft. After that she and her parents moved away from the apartment building and the kids all said it was because she had caught the rat disease; maybe she would even turn into a rat.

There were bombs in the airshaft where the adventurous bad kids and sometimes even Karpstein played. No warning, no air-raid siren; just a splat and a bad-smelling spray as a garbage bag bomb launched from an anonymous window somewhere above hit the trash covered ground. Larry McCormick got hit by a bag once and besides the stinking spread of coffee grounds and banana skins and other filth that covered him, he got a cut on his forehead from a bottle inside the falling garbage bomb.

Karpstein used his chair and two boxes to get up and push open the small frame of skylight. Then he pulled himself up and out onto the roof. The roof was his garden—a garden of tar and sand where nothing grew. He walked to the low wall around the airshaft and looked down. When the sun was overhead and the light shone down the murky shaft Karpstein could see broken bits of mirror winking among the bits of smashed tables, crippled chairs and fluttering rags.

The permanently abandoned belongings were picked over and whatever was too shabby to sell at auction was pushed through a large wooden door on the sixth floor that opened out onto the shaft. Twice since he had been here Karpstein had heard the shattering crashes as the unwanted was sent smashing down. The first time the noise had terrified him. Months later, when he heard it again, Karpstein found his way to the roof and peered down as the last items sailed to doom. Goodbye chairs—*crash*. Goodbye paper bags of assorted junk—*crash*. Goodbye once beloved icons of now disrupted lives.

Karpstein thought of tough Larry McCormick covered with stinking garbage, crying for his mother as blood ran down his face. The splat of the garbage bombs seemed only moments away instead of decades past.

Goodbye suitcase full of dead clothes—*crash*. Five or six flowered dresses, "house dresses" Karpstein's mother had called them, added patches of color to the scene. Someone had treasured them, had saved up for them perhaps, and now they were adorning a concealed pile of refuse.

When Karpstein laboriously let himself down through the skylight and returned to his room, his mother was there. She did not see him. She stood by the sink. He stared, but he was not surprised. In these private inner chambers of the castle of his exile there were few surprises.

She was not the decrepit mother to whom he had bid farewell in a run-down home for the aged a few years before. That mother, unable to hold either, leaked secrets and urine and complained endlessly to unseen listeners. He wrote to her, long letters, sometimes mailed, but usually not mailed, and tried to guess whether she was alive or dead.

The woman now in his hiding place was the mother of his childhood. Her back to the room and to him, she scrubbed and labored as if his tiny empty sink were buried under an endless stack of dirty dishes.

"Do you think I like it," Mrs. Karpstein whined, "to have to schlep from store to store looking for bargains just to make ends meet because we're always so broke?"

Theodore's mother, was always going shopping or to meetings. The speech was a familiar memory. It had been part of the preparation for almost every one of her shopping expeditions. Years later, when his father was long dead, Karpstein found out that while the meetings were all real enough, some of the shopping sessions were not.

She would primp and preen and leave the house—walking the long blocks from their shabby apartment to the bus station and ostensibly taking the bus downtown. Hours later she would arrive home, exhausted and edgy, with some few articles of clothing for young Theodore or his father and a housedress or some other item for herself. Homecoming was often accompanied by an almost theatrical retelling of how she was tossed about by crowds as she fought her way into Zearn's or Cline's or wherever the grand sale was being held. She loved to detail how she managed to get the prize for some incredibly reduced price even though dozens of other shoppers coveted the same item.

The tale, in all its many variations and episodes, was retold so often that Karpstein couldn't, in retrospect, imagine that his father never doubted its veracity.

He should have doubted. The shopping sagas were almost all the creative output of a frustrated wife. Mrs. Karpstein rode the bus downtown and shopped a while. But then she took another bus, walked a few blocks and rang a doorbell.

Mrs. Karpstein had a lover—perhaps several over the years. Theodore Karpstein, quite by accident, had found out about only one—a left-wing Jewish essayist named Milton whom she had met at a meeting.

So Sadie Karpstein got on the bus at least once a week to ride off to her tenement house tryst and come home filled with guilt and shopping tales of woe and wonder.

When his mother wasn't going shopping she was going to meetings. The meetings, meetings, meetings and meetings were sometimes a family affair. Big Al and Teddy and Sadie all rode the bus together to go to the meetings, except, of course when they were held right in the Karpstein apartment.

When Karpstein was young it never even occurred to him that the other families in his neighborhood didn't have endless scores of meetings in their livingrooms while the kids all played hide-and-seek in the closets, cupboards, bedrooms, playrooms, back porches, back yards or wherever else they were exiled.

To young Karpstein the word "party" had a very special meaning.

"Teddy, clean up your room," Sadie would tell him, "we're having company."

"We're having a party meeting is what she means," his father would correct. That usually led to whispered and eventually shouted arguments.

"Al, shaa! It's not necessary to announce."

"Sadie, don't shush me. In my own house I can talk."

"Your house has walls and walls have ears."

"I have nothing of what to be ashamed."

"Al, you're not in this alone and you don't have to shout."

"I can shout if I want to."

"You'll still be shouting when the *pogromchiks* break down our doors."

Pogrom was a word young Karpstein heard often. He knew about pogroms as soon as he knew about anything. Details of paving stones made dangerously slippery by fresh human blood—Jewish blood—and descriptions of a whole section of a city sparklingly carpeted with broken glass were often his bedtime stories.

The major story teller was usually his Zaida, the Yiddish name for grandfather. Zaida was a large, tobacco-smelling man whom advancing age could only curve, but not compact. A succession of cigars had painted a bright yellow path to his mouth in the snowy expanse of his unruly beard.

Zaida was magic. He could pull shiny nickels from Karpstein's ears and balance a cane on the palm of his hand and make things disappear and tell stories that made Teddy laugh until he had to pee. But some of Zaida's stories made Teddy cold with fear. They were stories of death drawn from real life. They were terrible stories to tell a child, but Teddy loved to hear them and, in his private world, experience them.

"This time we knew they were coming and we were ready," was the never altered beginning of the most gore-bespattered narration.

"It started," Zaida would tell him again and again and again, "when your Uncle Moshe who you never met—my son, Moshe who was killed by the Tzar and his *pogromchiks*—almost killed a soldier.

"It was *erev shabbos*—the evening before the sabbath—and everybody was getting ready to welcome God's special day. In the market the merchants was almost closing up to go home in time for *shabbos*. Pa, that's my father, your great-grandfather, may his soul find rest, had a shop with household and dry goods. Your father, my youngest son, wasn't born yet, but I was already married and had an almost grown son and two unmarried daughters and I worked for Pa. Twice a week I brought some of the goods by the market and sold."

Teddy Karpstein knew the story by heart.

"In the *shtetl* we didn't have much cobblestone streets. So on the dry days we had dirt streets and on the rainy days we had mud streets. So this day what should it be but a rainy day? I mean in some places mud up to the top of your boots.

"The market stalls had covers but that didn't fool the rain very much—you just covered things as good as you could and hoped the best goods didn't get too wet. Yussel the baker had the worst time of all. If my pots and dishes got wet, it wouldn't be neither the first time nor the last time. But with Yussel it was different because who wants to eat a soggy challah for *shabbos*?

"So this Yussel works out a way to cover his breads with a big board and then to put up a big piece cloth and tie it with a rope to one of the gateposts from the market since he was close by the entrance. It was that way every time it rained and that was fine by the rest of us and fine by Yussel.

"But this time came two Tzarist soldiers on patrol in the market checking that everything is just so. It was 'Pick up this' and 'Don't do that'—you know, enforcing the rules and seeing if they can collect a small bribe here and there. Well they come to Yussel and suddenly one of the bastards pulls out his saber and cuts the rope holding up the cover. 'Jew,' he says 'the bread may be yours, but the gatepost belongs to the Tzar.' And with that the other one give a kick and the whole table goes flying with fresh baked challah scattering into the mud. Everyone was afraid to say anything because if you provoked in those days you would get worse. So nobody says nothing and the hoodlums walk away laughing.

"Before I could stop him, mine Moshe gives a run and disappears. I knew Moshe was involved with some political gangs at that time, but I didn't know what he would do. I figured I just better pack it up and go tell Pa what happened.

"Pa, I should tell you, was one of the leaders of the *shtetl* committee and the committee was ready for self-defense. I, myself, was also involved in the committee, but I didn't really know so much from Moshe's gang.

"But before I could give a pack up of the goods, I hear such a tumult from the street that I have to run out and look. In the street just a little ways from the marketplace is one of the soldiers lying almost dead in the mud and looking like he just took a shower in his own blood. The other one has his rifle off his shoulder and he is pointing it up to the roofs from the buildings. 'Poom!' he shoots, but there ain't nothing up there but a couple birds flying away as fast as possible. What happened was somehow some loose bricks from the top just happened to fall at the moment the Tzarist bastards passed by and a brick just happened to hit mister rope cutter right on top of his head."

From here young Karpstein could have recited the blazing piece of family history right along with his Zaida.

The soldier didn't die...

"The soldier didn't die...

but the rumor went around outside the shtetl...

"but the rumor went around outside the *shtetl...*

among the goyim...

"among the goyim...

that he was dead.

"that he was dead."

No matter how many times Teddy heard the recitation, nothing could stop the chilled pounding it provoked in his chest or stop the sleep-breaking nightmares it kindled. He was there, small, frail and afraid. He was running for cover through muddy streets among toppled tables and angry people.

"I knowed right away it was my son Moshe,

may his soul find peace,

may his soul find peace,

and I was afraid it was all over

and I was afraid it was all over. I prayed right away to the Almighty to please let me see Moshe again in this lifetime. And my wish was granted. I saw him again—one more time. He came to me, his face all red and sweating. He was so excited. 'Pop,' he says to me. 'Pop, this is it. The revolution has begun. Please Pop, give the word for the weapons to be dug up.' Weapons? A few dozen glass bottles with stove kerosene. One single small barrel of gunpowder. Some bottles with gunpowder and nails and fuses. Small pottery jars filled with ground pepper and rocks to throw off the roofs at them. That was it. That and a few sticks, that was the weapons."

Karpstein knew the list well, through all of its insignificant variations. He was there each time. Sometimes he chose pepper and sometimes he chose bombs. When he felt daring he chose a pointed stick in his fantasy and fought them in the streets.

"Everything was buried in the ground in a root cellar under the courtyard of our house. Moshe knowed the place like he knowed his own hand. He could have got his gang, his young Socialists, and dug it all up himself. But he wanted me to give the order. What he wanted was my blessing. I gave it. Maybe I should have told him to run and hide and to get out of there. Nobody knowed he did it. There wasn't even informers who knew. But my Moshe couldn't hide and I couldn't tell him to run away. So by that night he was dead with a bullet in his *kishkas*."

Here was the accustomed pause while his Zaida sighed and a tear zigzagged through his wrinkles. Sometimes this pause would stretch into a long and silent reverie and Teddy would slip away from the story web that was being spun around him. Other times he waited out the minute, or five or even thirty minutes until the old man returned from the land of dead sons and fallen neighbors and resumed the telling.

The telling was their ritual; a secret handshake of man and boy connecting. It was a part of Karpstein's breathing and of his memory. It was an air-painted living mural of one prolonged scream—a scream of rage and outrage, of pain so bad it ended only in death, of horror so indescribable its only name was a scream. Not even the birth of another son, Karpstein's father, could make the older man lose his pain.

Karpstein was there. The walls melted away and he stood once again in mud. The *shtetl* streets echoed with shouting voices louder than the soldier's aimless rifle shot.

"The Jews killed a Cossack. Long live the Cossacks!"

The man was not dead and he was no Cossack. He was a simple, peasant recruit, but rumor-inflated myth has a tendency to gild its heroes and tar its enemies.

"and death to the Jews!!"

And the word echoed to the *shtetl*. The word, spoken and unspoken, murmured and only thought, that shook the walls of the clumped-together Jewish shops and homes, the word that made the rabbi, chanting the appropriate verses and prayers as fast as his quaking lungs could stand, take the sacred Torah scrolls out of the ark and hide them in a predetermined nest in the cellar. The word that sharpened the gloom of the *shtetl* was "pogrom."

"The *pogromchiks* are coming" was the whispered warning, the message passed from stall to stall, from window to window, the message that could clear the bustling street as easily as a wind hurries fallen leaves. And they came. Karpstein heard their angry curses. He smelled their torches and he smelled the acrid odor of his own fear. Karpstein, the boy at Zaida's knee, and Karpstein, the hiding man were one, watching the mobs surge through streets that should have been sweetly silent with *shabbos* serenity. The *pogromchiks* came, drunken on vodka and on hatred. They came carrying torches and heavy sticks. They came with rust-flecked sabers, jagged-edged from chopping at orchard underbrush, with shiny axes, with clubs, with crooked-tined pitchforks. With the half roaring inarticulate babble of any mob anywhere they came.

Pogromchiks, the half-affectionate Yiddish ending—*chik* as in *boychik*—made these feared and hated creatures also the object of scorn and satire.

His Aunt Rivka tried to make people see yet another picture of the pogrom warriors. She hated them, with the same jaw-clenching, trembling hatred as the others, but she wanted to explain them. Rivka, Karpstein's parents boasted, could speak to a street corner political rally without using a microphone and be heard even by the police spies hanging around like rats on the outskirts. At meetings in the livingroom of the Karpstein house her voice could make the windows vibrate.

"Yes, they were beasts," young Karpstein, banished with the other children to his parents' bedroom, heard her tell one such gathering "but who made them beasts?"

Aunt Rivka was educated She wrote pamphlets for the movement and when she spoke, she spoke her pamphlets. "These peasants were deprived by the landed class to the level of animals, besotted to the point of permanent mindlessness, and filled with a storm of super-stitions from the Middle Ages that made them see every Jew as a demon. They acted not on their own, but as tools of the ruling class!"

It wasn't until he was a teenager that Karpstein began to fully under-stand his Aunt Rivka's history lessons, but when he did understand his heart beat in rhythm with her roiling river of words about strikes, about labor heroes and about pogroms. He found himself wishing he had been there to fight.

"They were impartial murderers," his political storytelling aunt would tell roomfuls of entranced comrades. "They splashed roads and walls with the blood of old, of lame, of young, of rabbi, of fool and of infant. The masters and their priests made sure the peasants feared the Jew. The *pogromchiks* killed the Jew to protect themselves and the world against the curse of the Jew. The Jewish touch was evil, these ignorant raiders believed. But that didn't stop Jewish valuables, often drenched in Jewish blood, from crossing back across the line with the killers when they returned home. Jewish breath, they learned in their churches and their stenching taverns, could cause illness. That was no deterrent to the savage rapes that were the lot of any Jewish woman, whether unmarried child-woman or mature *rebbitzen*—rabbi's wife, who was dragged away by them."

Now, so many years later, the pogroms still went on in the rooms and passageways of Karpstein's building and his mind. He was there. Often they brushed past him, but Karpstein, trembling, embraced the shadows and was spared.

There was no stopping the churning swarm of destroyers. The gang of boys and girls (Moshe among them)who had taken up the hidden weapons were outnumbered at least five to one, but still they tried. Yes, there were girls too, skirts tied in the middle like pantaloons, who scampered across roofs to toss fistfuls of pepper or deadly rocks into the killing crowd. They struck and retreated. In alleys and passageways, Jewish sticks would be introduced to *pogromchik* heads. In seemingly unpeopled courtyards a Jewish volley of stones would go out in search of *pogromchik* Goliaths. A group of attackers on horseback were routed by flaming bottles of kerosene. But the fighters were few and their incidents of victory fewer.

In daylight the attackers were just peasants and townspeople. Soldiers were not involved since pogroms were not an official policy of the government. But after dark, uniforms appeared among murderous ghosts haunting the blood drenched *shtetl*.

With the soldiers came more weapons. Now a rain of bullets chased every mutinous Jew who dared to fight or even to peek out of hiding. Hiding was survival when pogroms were in the air.

Moshe was among those who refused to hide and now he was dead. An angry hornet of hot lead chewed its way through his intestines. His last words were "kill them, kill them." But they had killed him instead.

In a dark room, among dusty furniture, Karpstein lay gasping and watched his Zaida tell the story yet again.

"We had to hide to live," Zaida always concluded, "and you couldn't blame us. You'll see, they'll come again, you'll hide too."

V

Karpstein wrote letters to his mother and addressed them to the old age home where he had last seen her. He knew not whether the letters would be mailed, did not know whether Jews could still get mail, did not know whether the frail woman he had backed away from so long ago in a small room was still alive or could still read.

> *Mama,*
> *I can not tell you where I am. Mama, I am hiding. Mama, the pogromchiks came and beat me and Zaida said it was time to run and hide. Are you safe, Mama? Is there blood in the streets? Are the soldiers and the peasants hunting the Jews? Are there storm troopers*

where you are? Mama, are you safe? Mama, do you still hear and see? Where I am there is silence, but I can smell blood. I sit sometimes and wait for the sound of the boots on the stairs. Mama, I am hiding. I think of you. I have seen Bubbe and Zaida and also Papa. Dead people come to visit me. Sometimes I am afraid. Mama, are you afraid? Are you safe?

*   *   *

Dear Mama, I am so afraid. Please come to my room as you used to and tell me not to be afraid. I always listened to you, Mama. I am so afraid. I must not be found or I will be thrown to rot with the dead furniture. Mama, please don't let them find me.

*   *   *

My Dearest Mama, I miss you so much. Today the rats surrounded me when I came back with my food. Do you have food? When I saw you, you were washing dishes in my room. When I saw you, you were sitting in a chair and you didn't know me. When I saw you, I was little and Papa was alive. When I saw you, you were still alive. Mama, are you still alive?

*   *   *

Mameleh,
You were gone so much; gone so long. I needed hugs from you. You always left without saying goodbye. I saw you leaving and I cried. I am crying now. You always had packages. How many secrets are you carrying? I know your secrets. Are you my real mother?

ᘒ *VI*

Karpstein found another hiding man in his castle. It was a wandering night; a night when ghosts and Karpstein prowled the darkness together. Some old parts of the buildings were hardly used. Rooms stood barren of all except floating memories. Lights still burned on nighttime circuits, but only because nobody knew of them and turned them off. Like a shadow, Karpstein slunk along corridors filled with dust and shadows. There were too many rooms in the world of Karpstein to explore all of them. He entered those that called out to him or those he couldn't escape or avoid among the thousand anonymous doors in his prison palace. There were no markings on the door that invited him that night. An ancient hasp and padlock held it closed. But the hasp had been forced so strongly that the screws looked ready to

27

desert the dry rot wood of the doorframe. No pry bar marks had chewed the boards, but something had tried hard to open the door. Karpstein grasped the smooth handle and pulled. The screws still held their ground and tried to do their appointed duty. Karpstein tugged with more intensity. He tried rocking the door open. Push and then pull; shove and then drag. Again and again he tried. Each time the tired screws came closer to defeat. Ultimately they could not hold and, for the first time in unknown years, the old door opened.

Inside he saw dust and almost darkness. The dimness of the hallway light probed a tentative finger into the room. Above, a skylight much like the one in Karpstein's own hidden chamber, allowed a narrow beam of moonlight to penetrate. The room, although several floors lower than his own, was at the top of one of the maze of buildings that made up Karpstein's territory. The ceiling was much higher than that in his own rooms. It would take more than a wobbly, red chair to reach the roof in this empty place.

Karpstein was about to leave the uninteresting space and wander further when a shape on the floor caught his eye. In the dusky obscurity it looked like a sack of rags in the form of a person.

Karpstein crept closer to see the shape. He saw rags. He saw a shoe lying aside near the pile of rags. He looked again. He saw bones.

The bones wore frayed and torn pants and jacket. One bone foot was covered with a deteriorated shoe. The other bone foot was tied with a filthy rag that may once have been a handkerchief. Some dried flesh dressed the bones here and there and tufts of hair clung to a grinning skull with missing teeth and rotted teeth. Karpstein thought he should have been frightened, but he was fascinated. The bone person lay curled like a womb-protected child. A piece of thick hemp rope lay not far from the dry bones in Karpstein's valley of dry bones. Karpstein looked up towards the skylight. It was closed. A short piece of rope dangled uselessly from a corner so far above his head.

The rope had broken. The visitor tumbled to the floor. The visitor who had come to steal or sleep in warmth or maybe, just like Karpstein, to hide, fell into a locked room. The filthy bandage probably concealed broken bones on the bone foot. No ears heard cries for help in the empty nook of an uninhabited building. The hasp was forced outward by the fading strength of a desperate, hiding man. The padlock held tight as the starving, pain scorched man threw himself at the door. Karpstein looked closely and saw claw marks on the door; claw marks and dark stains that might have been blood on the whitewashed door.

Karpstein looked at the bone man on the floor. So many were hiding. Karpstein whispered "goodbye" and stepped quietly from the room of death. He closed the door and made his way, more weary than before, back to his room to examine the cracked and peeling mirror and see whether he himself was still alive.

VII

There was a monster in Karpstein's rooms. Karpstein knew about the monster, saw the monster, hated and loved the monster. Karpstein didn't like to call it monster because monsters are frightening and his monster in his rooms terrified Karpstein. Karpstein called it *momzer*, the Yiddish word for bastard. He called it bastard, "You *momzer*, you *momzer*, you *momzer*, you bastard, bastard, bastard, bastard," but it was still a monster monster monster monster monster.

Karpstein had run from his monster so many times, so many places. In childhood it had been monster-under-the-bed, monster-in-dark, monster-in-closet. In life it had been the monster, the bastard, fucking bastard of a monster that you ran away from and hid. Memory monster of *momzer* bastard memories breathing vomit stink fire smoke when the pain memories came to burn him. Run away and hide, but Karpstein was hiding and there was no more running. In his locked-in privacy of building of many, mutable rooms there was no running and when the monster became the resident, Karpstein was the visitor.

Sometimes Karpstein opened a door and the monster was there. Sometimes the door opened and the monster came in.

"There is no *momzer* monster," Karpstein said. "The monster bastard in my room does not exist," said Karpstein as he brought it a small bowl of water.

Twisted neck, scaled, horned head, flame eyed, jagged teeth, slime covered, color of wet silver, claw winged, thorny tailed monster was in Karpstein's room—visits were unpredictable.

"Bastard, fucking bastard *momzer*, you do not exist!"

The monster almost filled the room and Karpstein was crowded into a corner. He threw the monster a stale roll. The monster shrank.

"You stink of rotted shit, of sewers. You are nothing."

The monster groaned. Karpstein screamed.

Karpstein nurtured his monster. He threw it vegetables that he was saving for his own dinner. The monster nosed them aside and chewed off Karpstein's arm. The arm grew back. With splintery, fetid, monster teeth it gnawed off Karpstein's head and the head was still there. The monster opened its mouth and bit Karpstein in half. Karpstein was still there, intact, unscathed, but soaked in his own horror.

"Enough, bastard creature," Karpstein said and the monster sighed and disappeared.

Karpstein looked everywhere, but the monster seemed gone.

"He is inside me," Karpstein thought, "Inside me, always hiding inside me. In my rooms he is inside me, in my darkness he is inside me. When Mama turned on the light and looked in closets and told me to sleep again, monster-under-my-bed was always hiding inside me."

Karpstein turned his face toward the ceiling and let out a growling, roaring, howling monster scream for all the world to hear, but no one did.

⊗ VIII

Some of Karpstein's early memories echo with the words *party* and *comrades* and *workers*—almost always in conjunction with "fellow," as in *fellow workers*. His parents were both members of the Communist Party. They had met, they were fond of retelling, on a picket line. They joined "The Party" together on the same day they became engaged.

In his gloomiest and most frightened moments young Karpstein would try to console himself by saying the mysterious word "party" over and over again and telling himself that since his was a "party family" (a phrase he'd heard over and over again), life had to be one big party. The fiction didn't work, but children and the superstitious will try any and everything in an attempt to make their magic perform its prayed-for miracles.

Miracles and magic may have worked for some kids, but for Karpstein, faith was just "we can't afford it" another thing he didn't own.

All those good-luck, bad-luck bits of wisdom schoolmates passed on as solemn truths and the fingers-crossed protections didn't work for Karpstein. For him no hocus-pocus, voodoo mysteries could make school be over sooner, make him not get yelled at, or stop the pogrom young Karpstein himself witnessed.

Karpstein saw a pogrom—was, with many others, older and younger, forced to watch for months that drifted through the seasons and became years. It was a modern pogrom, watched by millions around the world. The old style pogroms, the ones that bled again and again in family lore, were watched only by the participants. In the old style, perhaps two hundred human blood beasts murdered two dozen Jews and then the pogrom was over until the next time.

The worst of violence is the threat of violence. When the smoke has cleared and the sacrificial blood has been scrubbed away, the haunting ghost of "next time it could be you—next time it could be worse" hangs in air, perpetuated by every echo.

Karpstein saw the modern pogrom and knew that next time it could be worse; next time it could be not him, but his parents. The modern pogrom killed only two Jews, but killed them a million times in newspapers, in newsreels, on radio, in magazines and on the gray and grainy infant, television. Millions watched and read and listened to every moment as the gang of Jews was rounded up and tried by a Jew judge who the modern *pogromchiks* had appointed as their kapo, as their special Jew among Jews.

The modern *pogromchiks* didn't say this gang of Jews had stolen a Christian baby for Passover matzoh blood. The modern *pogromchiks* didn't say this gang of Jews had poisoned the fields or killed their Christ. Instead, this gang of Jews was called spies. This gang of Jews, they said, stole atom bombs, they said, and, they said, gave them to Communism, they said, and everybody knew, they said, that Communism is Jewish.

Karpstein watched and in him a terror grew. The two Jews they would soon kill a million times in print and pictures and real life while the whole world watched had sons like him. Would it soon be his own mother and father who looked tired and scared and sad and resigned out of pages and pages and pages?

Karpstein, young, didn't always understand the details he read and saw, but at the meetings and meetings he heard it discussed and argued until he felt he knew the two Jews and their gang as well as he knew the people in the room.

He went to protest rallies where the singing, chanting, speech-listening crowds were so big he couldn't imagine that anyone was left to disagree. Karpstein carried signs and gave out leaflets. He went in a bus with his parents and most of the people who appeared at all the living-room meetings to Washington where they marched in front of the White House. Karpstein didn't see the President. Later he saw the Smithsonian Institution from the outside and his father yelled at him in front of everyone.

The protests, the marching people, the President didn't stop the two-Jew pogrom and soon, a million times, the Jews were dead. The Karpsteins, Al and Sadie and Theodore, and all the marching people crowded into trains and went to the funeral. The streets were full of people marching behind the funeral cars and young Karpstein marched and marched and marched with them.

Karpstein waited for the next pogrom to strike. He secretly knew his parents would be next. He waited but no police or cameras came to take them. Men in suits came to the house to ask questions. Big All shouted and cursed at them and they left. They, Big Al told the gathered comrades at the next meeting, were the sonobabitchFBI and most of the people there said, yes, the bastards had visited them as well.

Friendly neighbors tiptoed to the Karpstein door to tell of the same suited men coming to seek information. The suits were seen at the fur shop where Karpstein senior worked. They were everywhere. But they came alone. They never brought door-breaking soldiers or prison vans to carry Teddy Karpstein's parents to the electric chair. Even so, he never stopped waiting.

It wasn't pogroms, old style or modern that killed Karpstein's parents. Mr. Karpstein, Al, a furrier by trade, hacked and hawked and coughed and sneezed to clear the small bits of silky animal hair from his nose and throat and lungs for as long as Theodore could remember.

"Today we sewed mink to make coats for those dirty bourgeois bastards," he'd proclaim. "Tonight I'll spit up enough snot-covered mink fur to make a mink coat for you, Sadie."

Big Al, the furrier, the party member, went home from the party early. He coughed and hawked and ranted and shouted himself into a heart attack and one day he simply was dead.

Sadie never died. She just muttered in a white room and peed on herself and almost didn't recognize her son the last time he visited.

∞ IX

A familiarly acrid smell curled through the keyhole of a large middle corridor room on the fourth floor of Karpstein's world. He stooped to try to see its source. Darkness. The odor should have repelled him, but its familiarity beckoned.

The thick wooden door swung open with remarkable ease at his touch. The tangy odor rushed out to embrace him, but the darkness conspired to hide the rest of the room from him. Two or three steps into the darkness and Karpstein stumbled against a table. Something fell and struck the floor between his feet with an ominous *thunk*. His eyes and the darkness made their inevitable compromise and Karpstein looked down to see a long, sharp butcher knife stuck point first and still quivering. Two more such knives lay on the table, freed by his jolt from the brittle newspaper and rotted-to-pieces string of their wrapping.

He looked up and he was in "the shop." It was the land of mystery to which his father was always disappearing and, on return home, to which he was always referring. "You'll never guess what happened today in *the shop*…"

On his first visit seven-year-old Karpstein wasn't sure what to expect. "Maybe, it's like the butcher shop," he told himself. He went to the butcher shop with his mother. He watched the fat horse flies of summer grow fatter on bits of blood and meat while Sadie Karpstein bargained and wheedled for her family's dinner.

"My father makes fur coats and fur comes from animals," he had informed his first grade classmates, but he had no idea what that really meant. Perhaps the shop was a place where animals were cut up.

Now he was there again, the scarred, hiding man the young boy had become watching the scared young boy and the father who was dead entering the fur factory.

A buzzer sounds and Al Karpstein pushes open a barred gate and enters with his son. Young Karpstein looks around. There are no bloody carcasses hanging on hooks from the ceiling as in the butcher shop. Instead, there are bundles of furry skins stacked on tables, hanging on wheeled racks, and even lying on the littered floor.

"It looks like teeny weeny animal overcoats that the animals had just took off to trade in."

Karpstein, standing again in his past, remembered trying to imagine up what the animals looked like without these coats. He pictured them running about naked with little, circumcised penises dangling in front of them. Or possibly the coatless animals, dressed in stained white union suits of the kind his father wore, were dashing embarrassedly from hiding place to hiding place.

The smell, something between the neighbor's dog still wet from a bath and the urgent odor of cat piss in the hallway of his Aunt Zelda's apartment building, crackled in his nose and made him uneasy.

"This is my son, Teddy," roared Big Al to a black man who was pushing a rolling rack of fur collars.

"You looks just like your daddy," answered the man.

"Teddy, say hello to Mister Higgs," said Al.

"Higgsie is a comrade," Al whispered after the man continued on his way with the squeaky wheeled rack.

"Look, I brought my kid to see the place," Al told another one of the men.

"Well, well, sonny, are you gonna be a furrier just like your poppa?"

Young Karpstein was too overwhelmed by the noise and smell and new sights to answer.

"What's the matter with you, Teddy? Answer the man." Al simultaneously pushed his son forward and gave his arm a bruising pinch. Before his frightened son could respond with more than a stammer, Al answered for him, "No, this kid's going to college. He's gonna be in the leadership, not in the rank-and-file."

"That's good, that's good," the man told the boy and patted him on the head.

"Louie, look, I brought along my *kaddish*," Al shouted to a man in a cage. Religious Jews lived in terror of not leaving a son to chant the all important *kaddish*, the prayer for the dead, after their passing. For Karpstein senior the statement was just another loud-mouthed joke. The cage was a fenced-in cubicle in which the ermine and highest-grade mink pelts were kept. Cutters like Big Al who were working on special orders had to sign out their bundles of furs from Louie's cage. Theodore Karpstein stared at the man's arm. There was a strange tattoo there. Instead of tattoos young Karpstein had seen at the beach, a heart or a ship or a snake, Louie's faded blue decoration was just numbers. All around the shop, Karpstein had seen numbers, written with felt tip pens on the smooth backside of some of the pelts. Maybe this man's tattoo had something to do with that. Karpstein tried to imagine Louie's skin neatly cleaned and trimmed, hanging with a batch of others on a rack.

"Louie was in the camps. They killed everyone else, but Louie survived. Right, Louie?"

The other man nodded. He didn't smile or frown, he just nodded.

"They wanted to put all of us in concentration camps, those nazi bastards," Al announced louder than necessary.

Teddy didn't know what his father meant, but he nodded. He couldn't take his eyes off the blue numbers on the man's arm. He saw a five and an eight and a line of other numbers. One of them looked like a seven, but it had line through it.

"Hey Louie, show Teddy your number. They stuck numbers on people, just like meat."

Louie in his cage obediently extended his arm as if he were displaying a symptom to a doctor. Teddy stared. He reached out and tried to touch the numbers but the cage was between him and the arm. He didn't know what the numbers meant. All he knew was that they happened at "the camps." He wondered whether some of his school friends who had gone away to summer camps would come back with blue numbers on their arms.

*   *   *

The summer before his father stopped shouting for good Karpstein visited the shop one last time. Young Karpstein was in junior high school and, in the inevitable presentation ritual, Big Al introduced him as "My son Teddy the professor." Louie was still in his cage. Higgs had died and another black man, this one with one eye and no smile, pushed the racks of limp pelts. The shop was hot and the invasive creature smells clung to the skin. A radio blared in a corner of the shipping department and its tinny sound infiltrated the entire space.

Movement was everywhere. Torpid, lethargic activity, but so eye-filling as to seem like a whirlwind captured in slow motion.

A short, bald man with a drooping moustache approached them.

"Hey Teddy, meet Morris, our shop steward. He's a big shot in the union." Big Al's voice could not conceal a grain of bitterness in the description. Big Al had been the shop steward, but his increasing lack of diplomacy and frequent shouting matches led his comrades to gently edge him out.

"So how do you like the fur business, sonny?" Morris the shop steward asked, smiling benevolently at the progeny of the man with whom he had an uneasy truce.

By this point in his life Karpstein had his own shaky truce going with his father. In his imagination he had confronted Big Al with a screamed "I hate you" on more than one occasion. By this time he had learned that the animals who gave up their furs were really dead.

Young Karpstein knew what dead meant. He had found Fluffy, the stray cat he was not really allowed to keep in the house but had named and talked to and fed with stolen bowls of milk in a vacant lot behind the apartment house, dead.

The soft, gray coat was smeared with blood and crawling with flies. The greenish eyes bulged out and Fluffy's body was crushed and distorted by a car's wheel. For a frightened, distressed moment Theodore actually pictured his father taking the dead cat's furry skin and taking it to "the shop" to add to one of the smelly stacks. Before that could happen Karpstein put his semi-pet's squashed body into a cereal box festooned with crepe paper. With a ritual invented for the event, he buried the cat in the vacant lot next to their apartment building. Fluffy was put to rest under a mound marked with a faded paper flower swiped from a dusty bouquet in the family living room and a six-pointed Jewish star made of popsicle sticks.

Teddy wore a hat for the funeral, but not a yarmulke. In the street when he was alone he never dared to wear the skullcap that would identify him as Jewish.

The hat for the cat funeral was a cowboy hat his uncle Abe had bought him. Teddy had considered carefully. He knew it couldn't be official unless he wore a hat, but he wanted an out. He needed a covering lie with which to shield his sacred duty in case of an invasion by ridiculing parents or neighborhood bullies. He would tell them this was a cowboy and pirates game. He was burying the treasure. If anyone wanted to see inside the decorated cereal box Theodore would die defending it. That was the plot.

He walked slowly. One, he had observed, did not rush at a funeral. From the moment he left the urine-smelling hallway of the apartment building, he was chanting. He didn't yet know the real words, but he made up sounds that were a close approximation of the gibberish that both bored and fascinated him in his few synagogue visits. Slowly. Measured tread. *Ishkadah iskagah* (the mourners' prayer, he knew, sounded something like that.) *Borook attah nat illahs shama yiss roil* (*"Yiss roil"* was an important phrase, he decided—they said it often— so he sprinkled his funeral chant with a liberal ration of it.) The act of prayer, young Karpstein had noticed, also involved rocking back and forth and bowing from the waist. So he rocked and swayed and bowed until he was at the brink of dizziness.

And so the cat was buried. Fluffy is dead. Long live Fluffy.

In the shop the innocent son asked, "Why do they have to kill so many animals to make furs?"

Big Al's gasp was just a step below audibility. Morris, caught off guard by the question, just chuckled. "Uhh, that's a good question. Yes, a good question. Well, Karpstein," referring to Al, not Theodore, "I see why you call him the professor."

Morris walked away and the boy could feel dark clouds gathering. Young Karpstein had been through this before. He would sometimes deliberately taunt his father into this explosive state, but this time it had been accidental. A random word or action started the eruptions and nothing but time seemed capable of stopping them. The boy had been in the center of the storm many times. He had seen his mother in the center even more often. Even neighbors and strangers on the street, guilty of real or imagined transgressions, were not exempt from the spewing of his father's verbal volcano once they touched the unpredictable and invisible trigger.

Big Al, his jaws clenched tightly around the words "come here," led the way out through a fire door and into a grimy, dimly lit hallway just outside the shop.

"What's wrong with you!?" (The first rumble of thunder) "What the hell is wrong by you?" (Louder thunder)

A large hand grabbed the boy's shoulder and pushed him against the wall. (The first quick flash of lightning.)

"Answer me, you little putz, what the goddamned hell is the matter with you."

The thunder now was a continuous rumble bursting right in his ears. Lightning flashes, in the form of staccato finger pokes intersticed with shoves and pinches, accompanied. A sputtering rain of saliva and white flecks of foam swept young Karpstein's horizon as well. He winced.

"What the hell are you closing your eyes for? Look at me when I talk to you! What the hell is the matter with you, asking one of the big shots from the Furriers' Union why he has to kill animals? You want to make from me a complete laughing stock? What are you, the fucking ASPCA that you're so goddamned worried about killing animals? If you don't like how I make my living why do you eat in my house? Go somewhere else. Go get yourself a father that's a professor or a pharmacist or something if you don't like what I do, you little piece of shit. I'm sorry you was ever born!"

This was the eye of the storm. The thunder was deafening. The lightning slammed the boy against the wall. He started to cry.

"What the fuck are you crying for? I ought to knock your stupid head off..."

The hand that had been jabbing him and jolting him against the wall came up suddenly in a violent swinging movement. Theodore recoiled and threw his hands up before his face in an instinctive gesture of self-defense. In the quick reflex action one small hand glanced off Big Al's nose with a dull sound.

The storm machine stopped. This, the younger Karpstein thought, was the end. He cringed, choking on his tears, awaiting death. Now would come the ultimate punishment. Striking one's father was probably a bigger crime than murder and only murder—his murder—could be the penalty. Instead, Al Karpstein stepped back, put his hand to his nose and looked to see if there was blood on his fingers. There wasn't.

"Go downstairs and wait for me. I'll take you home," he said in a voice so subdued that one might wonder who had been doing all the shouting less than a minute before.

Theodore Karpstein went downstairs and waited. The episode was over. His father never in his life mentioned it again.

X

It was cold tonight. Karpstein, the hidden ghost in an attic cell, shivered under all the clothing and ragged blankets he owned. The shudders of cold made his stomach muscles clench so tightly they ached. His hands felt stiff and uncoordinated. He could not sleep. He stood up and pulled the string to turn on the bare bulb above the center of the room. Karpstein stood on the chair and warmed his fingers on the bulb. When his hands were warm his whole body felt warmer.

"I can't really think when I'm cold," he said out loud to nobody in particular.

Karpstein leaned his ear against a water pipe that he had wrapped with a cloth for exactly that purpose. It was his listening line to the land of people far below. They had all gone. It was quiet. He imagined he could hear the night watchman snoring.

"Lazy bastard," he muttered.

It was time for a walk. Karpstein trembled inside. The building was his private city, it was his country and his planet. In the building Karpstein was king and fool and ghostly wanderer through dark hallways lit only by the eerie glow of red bulbs above firehoses coiled like great sleeping snakes in their glass cases. When Karpstein walked these halls he was no longer prisoner.

The 2x4 was wedged tightly into the metal folding joints of the trapdoor's drop ladder. He put his foot against the piece of lumber and his back against the wall. It took slow and steady pressure. He liked to count the seconds and slowly increase the force until the wood was twisted free. This time, he decided, it would take ten seconds.

"1-2-3-4-5-6-7-8… OOOF!"

The bar came free early and Karpstein fell backwards. He took a deep breath and got up. The rope was next. He pulled at one side of a snarl until it was loose and then undid a tangle that neither boyscout nor sailor would call a knot but that Karpstein could recreate, right down to every loop and twist. A few tugs and the rough cord slid undone. Karpstein coiled the rope and stacked it and the 2x4 in their proper place. He unfastened a makeshift hook and the door from his frigid tower was unlocked. He pulled on a lever at one side of the spring and the trapdoor squeaked open. The drop ladder rode down folded until the door reached about 45 degrees and then began to stretch out like an old, arthritic arm creakily pointing the way to the floor below.

Karpstein took his red chair and carried it 11 shaky steps down the suspended ladder. He thought of Jacob's Ladder. Jacob, father of Joseph of the many-colored coat, Jacob who was named Israel after he fought with an angel, Jacob saw a ladder.

And he lighted upon a certain place and tarried there all night because the sun was set. He took of the stones of that place and put them for his pillows and lay down in that place to sleep. He dreamed a ladder set up on the earth and the top of it reached up to heaven and he beheld the angels of God ascending and descending on it.

When Karpstein was a kid and everybody at camp sang "We are climbing Jacob's Ladder." Karpstein used to picture Jacob, in patriarchal beard and paint-splattered overalls, climbing up a ladder on the building across the street from his house. The painters stretched their high ladders up against the walls and stepped skyward rung after rung carrying brushes and buckets of paint. Maybe Jacob was a painter with a ladder.

The earth where Jacob slept with a rock for a pillow was the promised land. *And behold the Lord stood above it and said I am the Lord God of Abraham thy father and the God of Isaac. The land whereon thou liest, to thee will I give it and to thy seed.*

Karpstein longed for some promised land for himself. he was of the seed of Jacob. He longed for even a rocky desert if he could be safe there. But Karpstein knew it was not to be. For Karpstein, running and hiding was the only way he could be safe. Even that had been given to him along with Jacob's promised land. *And thy seed shall be as the dust of the earth and thou shalt spread abroad to the west and to the east and to the north and to the south.* Spread and wandering.

The floor greeted his shoes and Karpstein was happy to be off the unsteady stairway. He put down his chair and lifted the bottom step. The aging but still effective spring made a noise like some otherworldly song and the stairway folded skyward again. It withdrew into the hole in the hallway ceiling that marked the entrance to Karpstein's hidden lair and the trapdoor slammed shut.

He took a quick deep breath. Karpstein hated noises. It was an unlucky noise that could bring the stormtroopers and their goose-stepping, door-smashing boots. There were pogroms out there. Karpstein didn't know for sure, but he believed it was true. An inner voice had told him to run and hide and now he was hiding. The same inner voice told him that the hunt was on and he was quarry.

A piece of rope dangled from one corner of the trapdoor. It was Karpstein's way back to safety. If he stood on his red chair he could reach the rope and pull his lifeline ladder down again.

Twenty seven steps along the corridor to the corner. Nineteen steps along the next hallway to a small, empty utility closet. That's where the red chair would sit silently and wait for him while he wandered through his building. The storage company had divided the floors into large rectangular spaces. Each of the rooms had plank walls and padlocked doors, but Karpstein had no difficulty entering the chambers and moving from one to another. Loose hasps often made the padlocks useless. Loose boards made walls into doors. Vents and shafts made the building and its forgotten treasures accessible to Karpstein when other methods failed.

Tonight he would not venture below the top floor, the one just below his attic cell, Karpstein decided. He often made such decisions, but sometimes dawn would find him deep in the heart of the building, many floors away from safety and in a panic lest arriving workers find him or hear the sounds of his anxiety-filled race home.

Step after wary step—the beginning of every journey was always the most cautious time. Past the dark repositories of tables deep in sleep, of fading pictures of people long dead, of books lost in thought, of beds aching to tell their stories of virgins enflowered, babies born and of dying souls drifting away like puffs of smoke. Karpstein paused and considered entering one of the rooms to explore and to listen but he went on.

Ahead of him, about halfway down the corridor, a ray of flickering, yellow light shone through a crack in one of the doors. He moved closer, silent as a shadow, and heard voices from inside. He edged quietly toward the door and pressed his eye against the crack. Inside stately white sabbath candles burned brightly in a three-branched candelabra. Karpstein suddenly remembered it was Friday night. The candles stood on a heavy dining table covered with an embroidered tablecloth spread with gold-edged plates. Two elderly people sat at the table. Their silver hair, hers knotted into a bun atop her head and his flowing from beneath a black skullcap into a cascade that included a full and untamed beard, seemed to glow in the candlelight.

Karpstein recognized the couple. It was his grandparents, his mother's parents. They sat there, in a circle of golden candlelight, at their sabbath meal. The greeting "Good *Shabbos*," rose to Karpstein's mouth but he stopped it on his tongue. He was surprised to see them there. The last time he visited them, Karpstein remembered, they had been in a compartment two floors below. This night he did not want to talk to them so he continued on his way. In life, the adored, rabbinical grandfather had frequently admonished Karpstein to "Be a leader. Work to be a leader of your people. Remember, your people first; worry about the rest of the working class later." Karpstein had absolutely no idea what it was that this man he called Zaida wanted him to do, but he looked appropriately solemn on these occasions and nodded assent in what hoped was a proper grownup manner. Now, so many years after Karpstein had said what he had all reason to believe were his final goodbyes, the Zaida and the Bubbe began reappearing and the new message was "Tiboreleh (a pet name they insisted on calling him), don't run away. Be a leader of your people. Find a way to be a leader."

His family, Karpstein decided, had a tendency to underestimate both the difficulty and the danger of any given situation. It was easy enough to command him to take a position of authority. The command, entreaty, request, suggestion was never accompanied by even the smallest seed of practical information as to how it was to be accomplished. In his moments of terror as a child—half dream half fantasy intervals—Karpstein pictured himself walking awkwardly to the head of some throng, carrying a crumpled note from home, and telling the seething assembly that his Zaida, mother, father, Bubbe had told him to tell them that he was supposed to be their leader.

✺ *XI*

"Karpstein, you ain't no leader. You may be many things and if you ask me, I'll tell you I don't know what they are, but one thing you really ain't and that's a leader!"

Karpstein felt sick to his stomach. He wanted to fall down writhing and vomiting and be carried away on a big khaki stretcher by corpsmen who would deposit him in some out of the way ward in the base hospital until he was discharged as a civilian. But he didn't fall down or die or puke his guts out on the baked dust exercise ground. He just stood there feeling humiliated while this neckless thug of a corporal bellowed at him in front of some 400 other flat-footed fools in soldier-boy uniforms. Karpstein had been set up. He didn't want to be a leader. He wanted to be anonymous and invisible and stay out of trouble like all the other enlistees who dragged their asses through almost three years of penal servitude called Army. But when the corporal announced he wanted five men to volunteer to lead small patrols on a work detail, the equally thuggish sergeant of whom Karpstein was terrified had growled under his breath, "Karpstein, volunteer" and Karpstein volunteered. Nobody else but Karpstein stepped forward from the rows and ranks of faces standing at uncomfortable attention under the fireball of sun. It must have been a setup between the two neckless thugs; yet another opportunity to torture and humiliate Karpstein. One spider bullied him forward and the other spider pounced.

Karpstein had joined the Army to get away from predatious creatures like that—and from himself. He wanted to escape the searing rage inside that erupted at taunts such as these. Karpstein had found out how much his anger-driven fists could destroy.

Here, under southern sun, the new discipline was working. Karpstein listened, but was not present.

Karpstein still remembered the welcoming speech he and 4 other awkward greenhorns were given after being ordered to step aside from the rest of the new arrivals at the sweltering Army base in the state of Georgia.

"Goldmark, Levy, Kornfeld (the cracker sergeant pronounced it 'Corn field',) Karpstein and Samuelson. You boys has got one big advantage and that is that you is not nigguhs. But you also got one fuckin' big *dis*advantage and that is that you is *Joooos*. Now you just stay outa mah way and do what yous told and we'll try to see that you get outa here in more or less one piece. Now DIS-missssed—that means get your asses back there with the others."

Kornfeld didn't make it in more or less one piece, He was killed in a "training accident" less than a month later. Goldmark, Levy and Karpstein did make it. Samuelson, envy of all the others, broke down under the strain and was carried away screaming and crying. He arrived at the base hospital with his nose broken. The official report mentioned his running into a wall while trying to escape. After a few days of evaluation, Samuelson was put in an isolation cell in the stockade. He stayed there until the swelling on his face receded. Karpstein's final view of Samuelson was in civilian clothing, being put on a bus headed north.

Karpstein stayed. He stayed in uniform for 29 months and 20 days. Troops came and went, but Karpstein stayed. He was trained to be a soldier. In hot southern sun Karpstein learned to kill. Karpstein, who had learned to punch and fight, but never wished to kill was taught to shoot, to bayonet, to choke, to blow up, to knife a mass of imaginary foes. Human beings were turned to things. Karpstein, was taught to shoot paper targets and to stab and mutilate stuffed dummies who hung just waiting for their straw guts to be pierced with sharpened steel.

Away from the dusty training fields Karpstein was educated, through more subtle means, to evade trouble. In sour southern air red-faced anti-semites tried to kill Karpstein—tried to make him die—tried to kill his spirit—tried to make him want to die—tried to make him not want to live.

Extra pushups for Karpstein, the Jew. Garbage detail for Karpstein. Hidden slaps and punches for the Jew. If there were, mysteriously, not enough weekend passes to go around, Karpstein and the other Jews, mysteriously, were the ones who spent the weekend scrubbing something, moving something or painting something. Karpstein, the boxer was strong, was not afraid. He learned to kill without learning to die and without dying.

When weeks of training were done, Karpstein was sent to sit behind a desk. His tasks were to shuffle papers, to keep the desk clean, to salute, to write simple reports, and to stay out of trouble. He did his job with such a degree of invisibility that even his tormentors forgot he was there.

He sometimes jotted poetry in a small notebook, but mostly read whatever came into his hands. At his clean desk Karpstein devoured books of all kinds. Tomes of philosophical essays were followed by trashy novels which were followed by familiar classics which were followed by whatever current bestsellers happened to find their way into the base library.

At the end of his time, when Karpstein received his 14 day discharge notice, his main concern was to finish reading the thick book he was halfway through and the smaller one waiting in the top drawer.

∾ XII

Karpstein in his building walked quietly. The hallway away from the candlelit chamber where his long dead grandparents held their Sabbath feast was illuminated only by the dim red emergency station lights and the yellowish gleam of a bulb that glowed feebly behind an exit sign. There was a cavelike quality to the gloomy hallway. In this light the walls seemed damp. Ordinary blemishes and discolorations on the peeling walls glistened with the imagined luster of cavern slime.

To Karpstein's frightened ears his steps, as cautious and quiet as he could make them, echoed like hammerblows through the building. These explorations were his private ritual. He was compelled to hunt for unknown visions even though he feared that doom stood watching as he walked and the Angel of Death waited, grinning, at every turn.

Perhaps he would return to the chamber where the Bubbe and Zaida welcomed the Sabbath and seek comfort from them. Karpstein turned and retraced his steps. He knew from past experience they would not still be there, but the fear chill from within and the night chill from without made Karpstein long for comfort and company. His kingdom was an uneasy place to survey this evening.

Karpstein felt overwhelmed. He had just decided to head back to his nest when a noise from below helped hasten his retreat. Somewhere in the lower reaches of the building a complaining gate was opened and a heavy metal clanging door was slammed. Above his head, in their rooftop pen, the sleeping elevator motors sparked and droned into life. It was near midnight. It must be the watchman making one of his infrequent rounds. Karpstein's heart was pounding. He raced for the corner where his red chair waited.

The indifferent guardian had wandered past on some previous trips into the building's guts and Karpstein had just stood immobile in some hidden niche until the intruder was gone. This time Karpstein was close enough to home to return. From the chair Karpstein could reach the dangling rope. He pulled the trapdoor open and the rickety ladder squealed as it unfolded for him. There was no telling on what floor the elevator might stop, but if it came to the top, Karpstein would be gone. He scampered up the best he could with the added ballast of the chair. Once inside he yanked the lever and the ladder groaned. The springs collected the spread out joints of the ladder into a compact pile—resting on top of the safely closed trapdoor. Karpstein was back in his nest. He encircled himself with his blankets and fought the cold until sleep came.

 *XIII*

Days passed like uncounted twigs swept down an unmeasured stream. Karpstein tried to feel joy at being home. The cold in his hideaway should have exhausted him, but he couldn't settle in for more than a brief respite. In the world outside it was the holiday of Yom Kippur, the day of giving and begging forgiveness.

"I have so much to be forgiven for, but I have no strength to forgive with," Karpstein told a corner of his room.

He paced his minute domain nervously, stopping to touch a wall or some object and then turning to stride away again. After a long while his restlessness prodded him into taking another prowling walk through the secret world of his building. He climbed the creaky ladder and dusty staircases. He touched accustomed walls and let his shoes whisper through familiar passageways. But the unfamiliar awaited him even in the midst of the familiar.

Had there always been a door there? It was a hallway he stalked often in his prowlings, but he knew no room here on the left where an entranceway captured his attention and some uneasy magnetism drew his steps.

"You don't need to know," he told himself.

He began to sweat even though cold drafts reached for him from the exit door and narrow stairway down the hall. This had started as an aimless wandering. He had enough food in his penthouse chamber. He had a handful of paperback novels, found in alleys on various food hunts. It would have been easy to stay in his nest and read, losing himself in the neatly woven intrigues and ricocheting bullets of a cheap spy mystery. He had actually started the slow drift into one of the novels when the restlessness seized him. Now he was driven by an urge to drop down into the building kingdom below. He wanted to go on—to keep moving from passageway to passageway, looking at old furniture and sensing ghosts. But an ordinary door—similar in appearance to most of the other storage compartment doors encountered in the building— would not let him pass.

Karpstein thought he heard a low hum of voices from inside the mysterious room. Occasionally a distant, muted laugh seemed to punctuate the hum. There was no lock on the door. A small piece of wood—to Karpstein it looked like a small bone—held the hasp closed. It would take little effort. A quick tug and he could open the portal, glance at the secrets of the room and go on his way.

"I don't need to know, I don't need to know, I don't need to know…," he chanted to himself half aloud.

But he needed to know. He tried to turn and walk away, but it was as if some invisible guardian of this door kept tugging at his sleeve.

More murmuring from inside. Karpstein put his ear to the door. A rustling sound from inside?

"What if it's a meeting?"

Meetings in Karpstein's childhood were serious affairs. Children were exiled to other realms and adults sat down together to murmur, drone, shout, laugh (but not too often), argue, mutter, harangue and orate. The meeting Karpstein tried to imagine behind the tempting door was not a party meeting from his childhood, but rather some more mundane and immediate meeting. Karpstein pictured himself thrusting open the door and walking in on a surprised table of storage company executives discussing some bit of storage building business. He strained to hear voices from inside the room but no words became distinct. Like siren song, the rising burble of human sound engulfed and enticed him.

The door moved easily but slowly when he grasped the handle and pulled. Karpstein expected a room, but no room existed. There was no floor. The walls were not visible—or at least the frightened onlooker Karpstein did not remember walls.

An enormous pit filled the space as far as he could see. The pit was filled with moving, writhing bodies—all staring at or struggling to get a glimpse of the newcomer who stood framed in the open door.

Karpstein stared back. He wanted to scream, to run, to squeeze his eyes tight shut before the sight sunk in, but he could not move, could not blink. The figures in the pit, he could not bring himself to call them people, were grotesque. The deep crater was alive with movement. The wormlike creatures in the shape of human beings were climbing over each other at the bottom, struggling up the earthen sides, standing on others who had fallen. Skeletons with fragile paper skin spread thin over protruding bones convulsed in a seething choreography of horror in the huge hole. It was horror, but the moving corpses were smiling. They were smiling at Karpstein—and waving. They were waving and seemed to be inviting him in to join them—into their terror pool.

Karpstein recoiled, but he could not run. At the first opening of the door the sound had rushed out to capture him. It was a cacophony such as Karpstein had never before heard. It was a clamor of laughing, chatter, calling, cackling. After the sound had wound around him tightly like a tentacle, a tentacle of odor rushed out to clutch at him as well. It was a smell of blood, of rot, of death.

It was death plus laughter. The bloodstained creatures, some naked, some in the gray and black broad-striped rags of the camps, all shared the same huge joke. One man spread open his bayoneted abdomen with his hands and howled, not with pain—pain was a thing of the past— but with hilarity. A woman clambered up on some others who had fallen and showed proudly the two halves of her baby. The crushed and maimed were there. They showed off their dismembered limbs and tortured bodies as curios; souvenirs of some event they'd all attended. The gassed and shot were there—the bullet holes forever fresh, the blackened tongues hanging, incongruously, out of smiling mouths.

Karpstein had only read of these corpses, heard stories of them and seen them in pictures. When he was a boy the whole family stared at pictures of these people. They saw them in the newsreels on Saturday trips to the movies, piled like so many broken dolls, up on the screen while a whole theatre gasped or sobbed. His mother was forever seeing her uncle's, cousins' and grandmother's faces in unrecognizable corpses as the shaking newsreel cameras panned past. Now Karpstein was meeting them all in person and they were smiling like old friends and asking him to come along to their carnival of forgotten dead flesh.

He felt his legs giving way under him. He longed for nausea to grasp him. To vomit now would be a blessed relief. He clung to the door and the door groaned under his weight. He pictured the door tearing free from its hinges and sledding wildly, with him still hanging on, down the seemingly endless slope of writhing bodies and into some yet unseen, worse maelstrom of revulsion in the center.

Karpstein pulled himself away from the hell gate and ran, disoriented, all thoughts of silence and safety scattered behind him. The flight back to the nest was made blindly. He didn't remember it, but once safely there he fell panting on his mattress. Above him, around him, in every corner of his most personal room, the slime-scaled monster was there, bathed in obscene laughter until Karpstein, sweating, screaming, sobbing, fell into a faint.

∞ XIV

God whitened the world where Karpstein walked. It had been cold, bitter cold. Wind burned and cut flesh with icy coldness. Now it was, comparatively, warm. The whiteness fell in big, quiet flakes. Endless falling. Nothing remained without a cap of white snow. Even the silent night walker named Theodore Karpstein wore a layer of white on top of the wool cap he had pulled low over his ears.

Food was harder to find in the snow, but easier to steal. Silence and safety seemed easier to come by. Karpstein walked his familiar alleys and side streets, slowly filling his sack. The world was white and comforting. There was a box of bread at the back of one store and cases of milk in front of another. A crate of cabbages and one of carrots were the treasures to be gleaned from at yet another place. Soon the worn burlap sack was heavy and Karpstein trudged through the never ending wall of falling feathers toward his hidden home.

In a narrow lane of warehouse offices he saw someone huddled in a doorway. Karpstein had learned not to be afraid of the concealed souls who, like himself, haunted the night streets. They shared the same dark world and the same dangers. Karpstein approached the still form. It was a woman.

"Have you enough food?" he asked her. "Are you hungry? Are you OK?"

Sleeping perhaps. No response; no stirring. Her stringy hair hung half in, half out of the collar of a tattered coat. A coat warm enough for fall, but not for winter. Even the shelter of her doorway hadn't prevented small heaps of snow from creeping in to snuggle next to her and keep her company. No movement. Perhaps sleeping. He would leave her a loaf of bread to wake up to. Karpstein leaned towards the sleeping woman. She looked young, younger than himself. There was a glint of light from under one eyelid. One eye was shut tightly and the other was open just a slight bit. But there was no glimpse of pupil looking out at him—only white. There was no steam of breath leaking from her lips into the snowy night air. Karpstein's pulse quickened. He reached one shaking hand forward and touched her face. Cold, colder than the night. He put a hand on her shoulder and shook her gently. Slowly, like some great thing melting and crumbling, the curled up woman rocked forward and, without letting loose of the grip her cold, stiff arms had around her drawn up knees, rolled over onto the sidewalk. She was not hungry. She was not cold. She was not breathing. She was not seeing.

Karpstein clasped his food sack to himself and ran as fast as one can run through drifting snow, until he was back to safety.

∾ *XV*

Karpstein was lost. He felt lost. He looked lost, but there was nobody there to see him look lost. Trees were there; trees that were all like other trees standing silent. Whistling, shrieking, chattering and occasionally lonesome calling birds were there. A snake and a rabbit were there but left quickly with only a startling sound as their parting tracks.

Wandering on the edge of flowers, wandering on the edge of thoughts. Karpstein forgot the pathway to his own mind. Karpstein had visions, he had fantasies, hallucinations, illusions, nightmares, dreams, dreams, dreams, dreams. Karpstein wandered inside his building and inside his own head.

One summer at camp Karpstein had gotten lost. He had rambled for hours in woods that became forests, that became jungles. Rabbits became bears in Karpstein's timberland. Sounds became tigers, became beasts, became deranged hermit ogres.

Now Karpstein was lost again. Had never been found. If he let his glance and mind wander, the bastard memory monster filled his room.

Outside the shelter, whispered the monster, the Jew war raged; had spread. The pogroms went on. Karpstein sometimes expected to slip on blood in the streets he prowled for food; anticipated seeing body parts carelessly strewn in his familiar alleys.

In his memory dreams he saw them. In his memory dreams he was running.

"Run Jew boy run."

In his memory dreams they caught him. He writhed awake in sweating pain as the Cossacks of his dreams and the bullying tormentors of his memory held him down and cut off his penis.

"It's cut anyway," they roared.

His Zaida had told him of seeing that happen. They called it a Cossack circumcision.

"Let me see your dick!"

"No."

Karpstein was terrified. His stomach felt icy. The big kid was around his own age—maybe a year or two older—but almost the size of an adult.

"I want to see what a cut Jew dick looks like. Show it to me or I'll knock you down and pull it off ya."

A second kid, Karpstein's own size, but exuding meanness from every look and gesture, backed up the big kid. They were in a hallway. The young victim searched frantically with his eyes for someone to come, to intervene. People passed on the street. If their glances strayed to the scene in the entry, they ignored it. Karpstein tried to edge past his persecutors, but they pushed him back to a dark corner.

"Leave me alone."

Karpstein pushed the big kid.

"Hey, he hit ya. We oughta grind his face into the wall."

The big kid grabbed him and spun him around, pinning his arms behind his back. Karpstein struggled, but couldn't get free. The mean kid grabbed at Karpstein's belt.

"NO, let me go!"

The big kid twisted Karpstein's arm viciously.

"You yell again and I break your arm, Jew baby."

Karpstein's belt was opened and his pants yanked down. He felt exposed, revealed, as if some sacred secret was being unmasked to strangers. They stared at his penis.

"Hey, the Jew boy got a big one," guffawed the big kid "but it's all smooth and round on the end."

Karpstein felt sick.

"Now show him yours, Larry. Maybe we'll make him suck it."

The terror in Karpstein's stomach rose up to his chest. He fought to get away, but the big kid's hands dug into the muscles of his arms. Mean Larry opened his fly and pulled out a piece of flesh. Even in his fright, young Karpstein stared with curiosity. It was a penis such as he had never seen before. Instead of the familiar, round-headed organ worn by himself, his father and any man or boy he had ever seen naked, this penis had a chimney-like tubing that tapered to a point with a small opening. He gawked at the strange appendage. So that was what was cut off. Talk of a covenant with God, of circumcision, of *Briss Milah*—it was all talk, but this was reality. He once had that pointed hood too, that chimney of skin—they all did—but for men of Karpstein's tribe it got cut off.

"Here Jew boy, suck it."

The big kid twisted him downward, pushing his head toward the hooded penis. Karpstein resisted. He squeezed his mouth and eyes tight shut. He could not close his nostrils and a strong smell of urine and unfamiliar musk clawed at his nose. He felt a warm blob of skin brush across his face and push against his closed mouth.

An icy feeling ran up his spine. This was the horror of horrors. The kids at school, far from the hearing of teachers, taunted each other with this act. "Cocksucker", "suck my cock", "eat dick!" And now he might be forced into doing it. At this moment the floor should open. All of life should collapse into some kind of heap before him. But it didn't Instead,there was a strange feeling of detachment. Karpstein struggled against some strange impulse to open his mouth, to allow it to happen.

Footsteps.

They let Karpstein go and pushed him against a wall. They ran toward the door. Larry was adjusting his clothing. Both of them were laughing.

Karpstein pulled his pants up. He was closing his belt when the silver-haired lady appeared on the stairs at the end of the hall. She stopped when she saw him.

"Hey, you goddamned kid, get the hell out from here." she shouted down at him. "You ain't got no toilets in your house you lousy bestards? You kids come pissing in this hallway anymore and I am going to call the police. Now get the hell out."

Karpstein didn't have to be told twice. He ran.

He ran after he had no need to run. He ran away from the fear, the humiliation; he ran away from the memory of a spongy wad of human skin—so much like his own but so different—being pushed against his lips. He ran away from his uncle by marriage on his mother's side Sol who had done the same thing to him once in the shower once only once.

Karpstein had gone to visit. Aunt Fayzie went out shopping. Sol stayed home to lounge around and watch television and entertain his visiting nephew.

"Teddy, it 's hot. You wanna take a shower?"

The idea of a shower in the middle of the day seemed strange to him unless you were at the beach or something. He didn't want to take a shower.

"Teddy, come on, take a shower."

Teddy was afraid to refuse the invitation couched as an order. He felt uncomfortable away from his home surroundings. His home was an island of familiarity. The outside always seemed like a jungle of other peoples' culture and customs and expectations of which he could be guaranteed to run afoul. In this house it seemed to be the mid-day shower that stood as a ritual to be obeyed.

Reluctantly, Teddy followed his Uncle Sol down to the bathroom. In a silence broken only by Uncle Sol's humming of snatches of first one and then another popular song they got undressed. There were few if any restrictions on nudity in the Karpstein household, but still Teddy felt suddenly very vulnerable getting naked in the small bathroom with his uncle watching him. Teddy tried to be nonchalant. He tried to look away from Uncle Sol's nakedness, but he couldn't. His eyes scanned the flabby, womanish breasts and the protruding belly. Below the folds of the overflowing paunch, growing outwards from a tangled bush of hair, was a penis that looked very much like Big Al's. To a nine-year-old boy it looked enormous.

Teddy stared. The pendant flesh was awakening. It stretched out and took on a firmer, more rigid shape. The color changed as well from a nondescript pink that white people called white to a blushing pink with a decidedly red cap on the end. Veins of darker red, almost purple, ran along its surface. Uncle Sol's manner began to change too. He became more agitated. He stepped toward Teddy and turned and the large penis brushed against Teddy's chest. The boy was embarrassed and tried to step back, but the sink was right behind him. Uncle Sol stepped forward, pushing the stiff flesh against him.

"Don't be afraid, Teddy, I only want to fool around with you a little bit." Uncle Sol's voice was hoarse sounding and he was breathing much harder than before.

"Come on, kid, touch it—just touch it."

Young Karpstein's mind was a rush of confusion. He felt afraid. He knew his uncle was asking him to do something peculiar and illicit. He didn't quite understand. His own private parts, as grownups sometimes referred to them, were something he guarded from the sight and certainly the touch of strangers. Teddy couldn't comprehend what his uncle wanted.

Uncle Sol rubbed the hard penis against Teddy's chest. Then he put one hand behind Teddy's head to hold it steady and pushed the solid organ against the boy's face. He tried to push it into Teddy's mouth, but Teddy clamped his jaws shut and resisted.

"Come on, Teddy," Uncle Sol was gasping now, "Just open your mouth. Just lick it a little."

Teddy resisted and struggled. He felt like he might start crying any minute.

Uncle Sol backed off. He changed his strategy to one of entreaty. "Come on, Teddy, don't be afraid. There's nothing wrong with this between friends. You're my friend aren't you?"

Karpstein was silent.

"Here, I'll even do it to you."

Now a surge of fear rushed over the boy. The man let go of his head and, with difficulty, sunk down to his knees on the bathroom floor. He leaned his head forward and took the boy's penis into his mouth. Karpstein was not prepared for what that would feel like. The wet warmth of the man's mouth seemed to radiate out over his whole body. There was an intense pleasure in the feeling. He felt his own penis growing stiff and rigid in the man's mouth. Uncle Sol rocked forward and back so the penis slipped in and out of his lips. Karpstein felt a dozen unfamiliar sensations. Even his pre-puberty body could enjoy the wild storm that was sweeping over it.

Uncle Sol stopped abruptly and pulled himself to his feet again.

"See, it ain't so bad. Now you do it."

He put his hand behind Teddy's head again. Teddy still resisted, but hesitantly allowed the warm flesh to push his lips open. The penis filled his mouth to choking. He felt like he would gag. Uncle Sol pushed in and out a little, but Teddy's tight jaw would not relax. The unfamiliar skin pushed against his teeth and made his uncle swear with pain. After a few seconds he gave up and began rubbing his hardness against Teddy's chest again. His rubbing became more intense and so did his breathing. He stroked his hand up and down the length of his penis faster and faster. Suddenly he stopped and took a clumsy step backwards. He groaned loudly.

"Uhh, uhhhhhh UHHHHHHHH!!"

Karpstein was terrified. His uncle's face was as red as the mushroom-shaped head of his penis. Maybe the older man was dying. Suddenly a thick, translucent substance spurted out of the end of the penis. Some of it splashed on Karpstein's shoulder, some ran down Uncle Sol's hand that grasped the penis, the rest dropped in gooey gobs to the floor. Teddy had never seen anything like that. The stuff that shot out looked like pus. He had seen pus when the doctor lanced a painful boil on his knee. The swollen, agonizing pimple had gushed forth its gooey matter and collapsed.

"See that," the doctor had told him, "that's poison. That could have made you lose your leg."

Maybe Uncle Sol was filled with poison. Maybe he would have lost his penis if the stuff hadn't come out.

They showered. A quick, silent shower. Everything had changed. Now Uncle Sol's penis hung limply in place and instead of pushing against his nephew he kept a distance away from him. Even in the small, glass-doored shower stall the paunchy man managed to soap himself and shower without touching the boy.

The man didn't speak until they were out of the shower and rubbing themselves with towels.

"This is our secret, right, Teddy?"

Karpstein didn't speak.

"We were just fooling around, Teddy. Promise you won't tell anyone."

Teddy mumbled a promise.

"I'm serious, Teddy. I want you to promise."

"I promise."

"You won't tell anyone."

"No."

Suddenly the agitated Uncle Sol returned. Only this time his excitement was edged with anger. He grabbed the boy by one arm.

"You had better not breathe a word to nobody if you know what's good for you."

Karpstein whimpered. "I won't tell anybody."

"You damned well better not. I have ways of finding out and if I find out I'll hurt you really bad."

He let go of the boy and pushed him away from him. Karpstein believed him.

"Besides," Uncle Sol told him, "it was your fault. You wanted it to happen. I saw the way you was looking at me. I wouldn't have started anything if it wasn't for you." Karpstein believed him.

"And if you say anything to anybody, I'll tell the whole family that you started it. Me they'll believe because I'm an adult." Karpstein believed him—because he was an adult.

∞ XVI

Maybe ten, maybe nine, maybe eleven years later, Sol was dying. The cancer crab had eaten his paunchy body thin. His pink skin was now yellow. Karpstein the young adult, who never breathed a word to anybody about the Uncle Sol incident, pretended that conscience or maybe family duty made him visit the clanking, groaning hospital. The sallow, needle and tube stuck voodoo doll that gasped and rotted before him in a room that stank of spoilage looked like no uncle of his. To the man who waited impatiently for final darkness to come, Karpstein looked like no nephew of his. Aunt Fayzie, also tired and sallow and almost beyond recognition, interpreted between the young man from the land of the living and the old man from the land of the dead.

"Sol, Teddy came to see you."

"Teddy?"

"Your nephew Teddy. Al and Sadie's boy."

"Teddy."

That was the extent of the conversation. Sol coughed and gasped some more.

"He can't talk much. They got him all drugged up," interpreter Aunt Fayzie explained.

"That's alright," Karpstein told her. "I'll just stay here with him a little while. You could go for a walk if you want."

She did want to. Fayzie was touched by her nephew's visit. She kissed his hand and simultaneously washed it in tears. She walked. Karpstein stayed. He pretended it was duty. What he really wanted was a word about the shower. Any word. Apology. Joke. Any word but silence. He got silence. Karpstein spent the minutes alone with his dying uncle pretending it was duty. Sol spent the last visit with his living nephew continuing to pretend—as he had at family parties and outings over the years—that it just hadn't happened.

"Uncle Sol, is there anything you want to tell me?"

"Fayzie?"

"She went for a walk. She'll be right back. We're alone now. Do you want to say anything?"

Long silence.

Aunt Fay returned and kissed her nephew's hand again.

"You're a good boy Teddy. Don't be a stranger. When Sol gets out of here, come visit us at the house. You haven't been there since you were a little boy."

"At the house…" Everybody could pretend.

Before the week was over Uncle Sol was dead. No apology, no word, no joke, just death.

∞ XVII

Running. They were running in the park. Danny looked at him with disbelief. "A *boxer*? Karpstein you got to be out of your fucking head. You mean like serious? Like a prize fighter?"

"What are you, in training or something?" Danny kidded him once or twice, when the running sessions first began. During this particular session Karpstein told him what he was training for. They were both 23 and worked in the same warehouse. They both tossed loaded crates on and off trucks with the same vigor as the rest of the crew.

Karpstein kept his even pace unchanged. He was serious. He had thought about it and he was serious.

"Karpstein, who ever heard of a Jewish boxer? Teddy, the *goyem* will laugh you out of the ring—if they ever let you get into the ring in the first place. What will your nickname be, 'Kid Kike?' Are you crazy or what?"

Danny Lyon (it had been DeLeon when his family, Sephardic Jews, came from Spain to America and changed it) was Teddy Karpstein's closest pal. The heavy duty verbal barrage was typical of the way they talked to each other. Karpstein didn't let the insults and mock insults get to him. It was just Danny's way of discussing. They ran together in the park a few times a week. They ran until Danny, his breath feeling hot enough to scorch his lungs, refused to go further. On the days Danny didn't run, Karpstein ran alone.

There had been too many beatings and too many scares. Around the time he turned 16 Karpstein had decided his bookish demeanor and scrawny frame were disadvantages he could do without. His strength building routine started out as part fantasy and part reality. He used volumes of the encyclopedia as dumbbells at first; holding them down at his sides and slowly curling his arms up until the books were alongside his nose. To Karpstein's surprise his body began to change. The muscles in his arms grew rapidly. He switched from books to bricks after a few weeks and also developed devices to use for exercising his legs and back. The newer Karpstein swaggered more and could not be pushed without pushing back.

*   *   *

Sadie Karpstein's first reaction to the whole warehouse world was even stronger than Danny's greeting of the boxer news.

"A warehouse? You're going to get a job in a warehouse?" His mother was at her whining, raspy best. "Your father worked himself into an early grave with the hope that you'd go to college and make something of yourself."

Karpstein was ready for her arguments. "College is not where the proletariat is. The proletariat is in the warehouses. Besides," he bargained, "I can always go to college later. Maybe in the evenings." Karpstein, wisely, never even considered telling her about the boxing plans.

In the end comrade Sadie Karpstein couldn't counter her son's arguments. She had to admit that extra money coming in would be helpful. Big Al's "death benefit" payments from his furriers' union pension were good, but they didn't cover all their expenses. Her dour-faced lover, Milton-the-essayist, who read his lugubrious tracts at the slightest hint of an invitation, disappeared soon after Al coughed and ranted his last. The prospect of Sadie's full-time availability didn't fit into his plans and he went on to lay with some other willing wife who was not and would never try to be his own.

College, she reasoned, was expense and a warehouse job was income. So at 19 and a half, Theodore Karpstein went and joined the proletariat in a warehouse. He had been working out regularly and he was strong. He had also gained a modicum of street wisdom. He was ready, he thought, for whatever the world pitched his way.

The world, for its part, didn't throw too much. The warehouse workers weren't ready to be organized, proselytized, convinced or converted. That actually didn't bother Karpstein all that much since the dose of idealism he used with his mother was more a maneuver to convince her than any kind of glowing dream. At times Karpstein did lapse into a moment or two of low grade rhetoric or preachiness about some radical precept but his efforts met so many polite nods and glazed looks that he eventually stopped trying.

In the blustery fall there was a "labor action" —not really a strike and not really not-a-strike either. Karpstein's surer presence was one of those on the menacing looking front line when some hire thugs showed up to try and intimidate the workers. Unfortunately, Karpstein was also front row stuff when the cops came 'round.

The restraints were on for the workers. Violence was the last thing desired by them. The beefy boys from the so-named "labor unrest" squad thought otherwise. For them it was a nice, brisk day for action. Karpstein turned his head in time to see a big, round-housing fist flying his way. Karpstein's newly acquired boxing skills had by that time sunken in deep enough under his skin for him to duck and bob even as a reflex. Seismoid bones scattered like skin-enclosed marbles as cop-wrist fractured, as cop-fist sailed through empty air where Karpstein head had been and hit brick wall where Karpstein wasn't. He wasn't even near that spot by the time the pain flooded up from wall to cop fist to cop wrist to cop arm. Karpstein ran for his freedom because he knew, if caught, his opportune ducking could cause his arrest for assaulting a policeman. By the time the other guardians of the peace realized what had happened, Karpstein was uncatchable.

What Karpstein enjoyed more than politics was his new found physicality. He ran, he lifted weights and he fantasized how much more impact his words would have if he could become a well-known professional boxer.

As a kid he had heard the hours of dreary discussions and speeches echoing through one interminable meeting night after another. Even the exciting speeches, the ones out in the parks or on street corners when the orators shouted and waved their arms a lot and when mounted policemen rode in to disperse the gathered crowd, were just noise. Karpstein never believed any new people came to listen. All the faces were familiar. His parents seemed to know everyone in "the movement" by name. There was more talk about people "dropping out" or dying than about new people joining.

On the other hand, he had once seen a real boxer live, in the flesh. It was "Jersey Joe" Walcott, a black man. And when "Jersey Joe" spoke, everybody listened. There were reporters with notebooks shouting questions at him about something called "The Battle of the Century" and they all wrote down every comment the boxer uttered. If a black man could earn the right to be listened to just by hitting people, then so could a Jew.

Karpstein started going to a rundown den of athletic activities and athletic smells called the 12th Street Gym a few nights a week after work. He kept to himself a lot and watched and copied. There were enough want-to-be and once-was boxers in the place for Karpstein to develop a fairly good training routine just through observation. He did sit-ups, jumped rope, learned to play a machine gun rat-a-tat on a light punching bag and to slug a heavy one until his fists and wrists were sore. After a while one or two of the other hopefuls who trained there noticed him and asked him to work with them.

The first thing Karpstein learned was that observing boxers in the gym, in the ring or in the movies did not teach one boxing technique. It took a few hours of ringing in his ears and a couple of puffy eyebrows to teach him valuable lessons about keeping his guard up and dodging out of the way of incoming leather. Soon he was bold enough to ask some of the other sweaty denizens of the gym to spar with him as well. It wasn't always easy. Quite a few of the regulars in the gym, foul-mouthed types with rattled brains and sullen, pushed-in faces, were very open about their aversion to working with Jews.

Once he convinced an ugly thug named Klaus Bruhn to spar with him. Sparring is not boxing. Sparring is a cooperative exercise in which two boxers put their skills to work. Bruhn was heavier than Karpstein. His bulky body told more stories of evenings spent swigging beer than hours spent training. Karpstein just wanted someone to work with and he knew from watching that Bruhn could box well. They put on the obligatory padded helmets and rubber mouth guards and stepped into the ring that stood in the gym's largest room. Another boxer came over to watch.

"OK, ready? Bong!"

Karpstein moved in cautiously. He was working on his jab-and-block combination and that was what he wanted to practice in this session. He flicked his left glove out and back a few times—sizing up his target. Bruhn moved forward with some strong punches. Karpstein blocked them and stepped back. Bruhn charged toward him and locked Karpstein into a clinch. A clinch is normally what a hurt or tired fighter used for a moment of recovery. Bruhn had other uses for the clinch. His belly pressed against Karpstein. THUD! A gloved fist walloped Karpstein in the area of his kidney. It hurt a lot and a wave of nausea followed. Karpstein was stunned, but Bruhn wasn't done with him. A sharp elbow hit Karpstein in the ribs as he tried to wrestle himself free from Bruhn's grip. He managed to pull clear and as he did a row of glove laces was rubbed across his eyes. The boxer who had acted as starter and observer was laughing. "Give it to him, Klausey," he encouraged. Bruhn needed no encouragement. He seemed to have a full repertory of fouls to show the less experienced boxer.

Karpstein's vision was blurred but he could see Bruhn lumbering towards him. Karpstein managed to sidestep, slamming a hard right hand into Bruhn's gut as he did. The larger man was slowed—shocked. Karpstein was angry. He had been fouled severely. His eyes burned and there was a dull aching in his side. He wanted to stop the sparring session before he got hurt even worse, but Bruhn was stalking him. Karpstein dodged and danced. Karpstein decided he had to make Bruhn quit. It took two fast punches to the head to accomplish that goal. Bruhn stepped backwards, wobbled and fell. Karpstein went over and helped him up, ignoring the scorching, hateful look that shot his way. Then he left the ring and headed to the locker room. Karpstein knew when it was time to steer towards home. It was dark when Karpstein left the gym. As he passed the alley next to the building, Bruhn and a gang of his friends were waiting. Karpstein kicked one of them in the nuts and ran like hell.

That week Karpstein changed gyms and persuaded Danny Lyon to come down and train with him at the new place. Lyon and Karpstein ("Danny the Yid" and "Kikey Karpstein" they were called behind their backs) became sparring partners at the McGraw Gym, just a 20 minute jog from the warehouse.

* * *

Three fights at $50 each was the length of Karpstein's boxing career. It was actually four fights, but he left the last one early. The fourth fight took place in a seedy former warehouse in an appropriately seedy part of town. The semi-improvised ring lights took on a yellow cast in the cloud of tobacco smoke that looked like it hung over the ring without subsiding from one week to the next.

About 300 paying fans bellowed for blood from opening to closing bell in a series of matches between pair after pair of boxers. Most of the worthy gladiators wouldn't have made even the preliminary warmup bout in an arena of even slightly more class. A few were beginners like Karpstein and one or two others were "up-and-coming", a term many of them clung to and mumbled between permanently puffy lips long after "has-been" was the kindest thing you could say about them.

Karpstein was scheduled to trade leather with a ruddy-skinned Pole named Philly Borek. They had never met except for a perfunctory nod and handshake when they signed in at the office before heading to the locker rooms. The auditorium's entrepreneurs, probably inspired by previous problems, provided two locker rooms and arranged for opponents on the evening's boxing card to be segregated until called to the ring.

"Braaaaap, " a mean-sounding buzzer snarled

"Ready?" Danny Lyon was Teddy's second. He checked the lacings on the gloves one last time. Karpstein nodded. The crowd noises, like several hundred men and a handful of women babbling together in strange tongues, echoed up the hallway from the chair filled warehouse where the ring stood. The air was pungent with a mixture of cigar smoke, beer and sweat. The bout before the Karpstein/Borek matchup had been boring—more like ballroom dance than boxing—and the crowd was beginning to lust for excitement. Danny opened the door and he and Teddy walked down the hallway together.

Just before they reached the makeshift arena, the place erupted in raucous cheers peppered with scattered boos. Borek was a local favorite and he had just started down the aisle toward the ring. Part of the crowd started chanting "Philly, Philly, Philly, Philly."

Just before Karpstein and his second came into view one voice shouted out "Hey Philly, you gonna win?"

"Yeah," Borek boomed back, "I'm gonna kill me a little Jew meat tonight."

The crowd response was laughter and more cheers and a swelling chant of "Philly, Philly, Philly, Philly."

If Danny felt a wave of terror, he tried not to let it show to his pal, Teddy. Karpstein's face didn't change except for a slight tightening of the jaw. His hands trembled slightly, but they always did before a fight.

When the crowd saw Karpstein, the boos and cheers were about evenly balanced. Sometimes there had been anti Semitic taunts hurled by anonymous voices, but not this time. In fact, the crowd seemed somewhat subdued, as if Borek's shouted insult had stunned and perhaps embarrassed them.

Looking back, Karpstein didn't remember the walk down the aisle or the climb through the ropes and into the ring. Borek's face grinned at him through a haze. The referee gave instructions, but the words were meaningless syllables to Karpstein. Borek's second and Danny both left the ring, but Karpstein didn't see them go. He saw Borek and he heard the bell.

Borek danced in gingerly; feeling his way with light, probing left jabs. Karpstein shoved the jabs aside and began punching. His first shot, a hammering right, caught Borek in the ribs.

The crowd, served up a promise of the action they had hungered for, came to life like a howling beast. Like Karpstein they didn't take time to work themselves up to a fever pitch—they started there. If the first punch caught Borek by surprise, the hailstorm of heavy leather that followed threw him into a state of shock. The crowd was in a frenzy.

Borek tried to block, but he couldn't seem to figure out where the next stinging blow was coming from. He held his arms in front of him in a clumsy attempt at blocking, but the barrage of punches that flew toward him crashed through that uncoordinated barricade and slammed against his flesh unhindered.

There was no emotion showing in Karpstein's eyes—just an icy reflection of the ring lights. Borek tried to fight back. He landed a few hard blows of his own, but his opponent seemed not to feel them. Not one person in the arena was seated now and not one was silent. It looked like Borek wanted to turn and run. He wanted his second to throw in a towel. He tried to get Karpstein into a clinch and stop those punishing arms for a few seconds, but there seemed to be six arms instead of two. Blood ran from Borek's nose. His mouth guard, a bloody piece of pink rubber lay in the middle of the ring. Borek tried to back away but a left hook to the side of his face and a hard right hand to his jaw made him walk crooked steps as if the room were spinning.

Then Borek stood there, melting slowly like a wax figure. He could not fall and he could not move. The crowd screamed in perfect imitation of damned souls in an antechamber of hell. Karpstein threw fists at the sagging form with a fury they had never before seen. At last Borek fell. The hysteria stopped. The crowd grew silent. The referee tried to count to ten but knew it was unnecessary and could not find his voice.

Karpstein didn't wait to hear the results announced. Hecharged up the aisle and into the dressing room. No one tried to stop him. He disappeared into the night.

Borek didn't die. He lay in a coma for two months and awoke, like Rip van Winkle, as an old man. He could feed and dress himself, but needed help with almost everything else.

∞ *XVIII*

Nothing had changed. Nothing was different. Stones, punches, insults, taunts: Karpstein had eaten insults, had swallowed punches, had held stones and taunts fermenting deep inside his gut and now he had spewed it all out of himself. In a puny arena, in the presence of his enemies, Karpstein vomited forth a binge's worth of ingested hate and pain all over one symbolic Jew killer enemy.

"So nothing has changed," Danny Lyon told him.

"I know, but I won."

"You won."

"I beat him."

"I never saw you so mad."

"What are you trying to say, Danny."

"I ain't trying to say anything, I just never saw you so mad."

"Yeah, I was mad. I was fucking mad. Did you hear what he said?"

"I heard what he said."

"So what would you have done, kissed him?"

"Fuck you."

"Fuck yourself, Lyon. What the fuck would you have done?"

"I would have beat the crap out of him."

"What the fuck do you think I did? I beat the fucking crap out of him."

"Teddy, you fucking near killed him. If you had had an axe in your hand you would have chopped his head open and stamped on his brains all over the ring."

"What difference does it make? He deserved it, he's a fucking anti-Semite of the worst fucking kind."

"That's what I mean, Karpstein, it doesn't make any difference at all. When you went in there you didn't even see Borek. He didn't even exist for you. You wasn't fighting one anti-Semite, you was fighting every fucking anti-Semite in the world who ever threw a stone at you or cursed you and maybe a couple of those insane, wild punches were aimed at your old man, Big Al, too."

"And?"

"And nothing has changed. Nothing except that Borek is in the hospital and he might die. I can just see it 'Jew boxer kills opponent for cursing.' Nothing else has changed. Big Al was dead and he's still dead. You're still a Jew and the anti-Semites are still calling you a kike and throwing stones at little Jewish kids."

"What the fuck, Lyon, did you find some dollar ninety eight psychology book in the toilet or something?"

"Eat shit and die, Karpstein. Go get your fucking axe and split some heads. Maybe you'll go down in history as the Jewish Superman or something…or maybe as the next Golem."

"Go to hell, you lousy bastard!"

Teddy threw a shoe at Danny, but Danny was gone—for a long, long time. Karpstein stood, surrounded by his demons. His anger had been ejaculated and he was weak and dizzy.

Nothing had changed. Nothing was different. The demons were still there. Two weeks later Karpstein signed a paper agreeing to become a member of the U.S.Army.

∞ *XIX*

Karpstein knew he would prowl out into the sea of cacophony that night. The building was filled with sounds that called him. Outside, the wind blew the clouds off the face of the moon and sent empty cans scurrying clamorously through streets and alleys. Inside, the pipes moaned and floors creaked. Other, unidentified, voices joined them.

The ladder from the nest creaked like some insane cello in a symphony of dissonance. Karpstein's footsteps echoed percussion. The wind across the pipes and openings played atonal tubas and shrieked the arpeggios of dying sopranos. The walls unloaded murmuring voices as Karpstein drifted along corridors, through doorways, down haunted flights of stairs—pulled as if by some hidden tractor beam. Familiar

spaces; the unused decay of some dusty bygone office, an alcove ending
in a door—loosely nailed shut but easily openable. Beyond the door a
trash-cluttered staircase led to storage spaces only Karpstein knew. Now
stacks of decomposing newspapers, some with dates from before his
birth, were the only items stored there.

The moon stabbed between decaying boards like silver knives as
Karpstein walked to a rendezvous he had dreamt of and dreaded for
days. In the last room on this level of the neglected wing the light was
not silver of moon, but gold of dim light bulb. In the glow a man was
pacing. His shoulders were rounded as if awaiting the delivery of some
large weight. His steps, the reluctantly shrunken gait of one who had
expected the impatient stride of youth to go on forever.

Karpstein knew the man at once. Big Al had come. There had been
so many other visitors chatting, chattering, admonishing, advising
Karpstein. So many faces from so many different pasts had intersected
Karpstein's vision and confused his present, but Big Al had never, not in
dreams and not in wanderings, come.

Karpstein stared. He knew and didn't know this man. *I never noticed
how tired he always looked.* The big hands were laced with shiny scars.
The fur knife often slipped. Karpstein remembered seeing the red
marks, some not quite healed, when he leaned forward to see the waxy
figure that had been called father lying in a burying box. He wondered
then why they hadn't covered them with magic makeup. His childlike
idea at the time was that undertakers restore and even create perfection
for that last glimpse, that final public appearance.

Even in death, Big Al had the last laugh. Lying immobile without a
shout, an order or a slogan he still was the subject of controversy.

"Why is the coffin open? At a *Jewish* funeral?! It's a *shonder* on the
whole family." Uncle Ben rolled the Yiddish word for shame out of his
mouth like a biblical pronouncement. Ben was religious only on
public occasions.

"A religious funeral for Al Karpstein he wants?" A close friend of the family who was a comrade, asked nobody in particular. "What kind of a crazy person wants such a thing? If you do it, Karpstein will get up and walk away, I guarantee it."

The argument raged back and forth as theme and variations with Sadie Karpstein's piercing "Al, Al, why did you have to die?" as counterpoint until a certain Aunt Goldy, the oldest in the shrinking family, made her entrance and provided a closing crescendo.

Eighty-eight year old Goldy, a spirited woman called feisty by some and abrasive by others, was a life-long radical who had been to Moscow and claimed to have met Lenin. When she entered, her sure steps making the cane she carried look more like a stage prop than a support, there was a momentary hush.

She stopped and scanned the pseudo-plush trappings of the non-denominational funeral parlor, velvet drapes, upholstered mourners chairs and waxy-looking flowers, and said, to every ear in the room, "Oy, it looks like a whorehouse in here."

∽ XX

First was the hospital. Karpstein sat next to his mother's bed. Hysteria. She had heart pains—or something that felt like heart pains. So they gave her medical rest in a needle and let her recompose through sleep. Not far away from the room where his mother slept, also slept his father—in an antiseptic, refrigerated vault. Young Karpstein sat for a while, dazed, restless, watching this strange woman who was his mother sleeping with wires attached to her, and then they sent him home to a neighbor's house.

There had been rumors at school that his father was dead even before his father was dead. A neighbor from upstairs, Mrs. Krebs, not a comrade, came running to the school to get him. With the junior high school principal as her guide she burst into his classroom and blurted, "Come quickly, your father is dying." By the time the day was over the distorted story around the school had a policeman coming to get Karpstein to tell him his father was dead. "They always send a policeman," one of the rumor bearers related with knowing solemnity. A few of the more imaginative added a dreadful accident as the cause.

The dreadful accident was life. Allan Morris Karpstein died because life was too big for him to continue carrying. He died of shouting. He died of living. He died of politics. He died of rage. He died.

At the funeral home young Karpstein touched the hands. Cold. Maybe this was just a mannequin and his real father was standing somewhere watching it all—a joke, a Big Al joke. But it was real and he knew it was real. Later alone in the room where his father—still his father even though dead—was lying, Theodore, son of Al, looked closely at his dead father's face. A drop of liquid had run down the face from the corner of the mouth and down toward the ear. Its track was etched in the layer of makeup the undertaker had applied. "Happy Halloween, papa," young Karpstein said, in his mind, to the immobile, painted face that looked like his father, suddenly flooded with benevolence. Teddy was trying to lighten up the wave of confusion and heaviness that pressed down on him with a private joke.

His father was lying in a plain wooden box. "Al wanted it that way to show solidarity with the Working Class," his mother explained, using curves of her voice to let the capital letters of the last to words be heard. Another drop of liquid, maybe a tear, he thought, ran from the corner of one eye and down the cheek. The heavy wave was heavier. Teddy felt like crying too. His father was crying. Karpstein, living son of a dead father, reached out and touched the face of Karpstein, dead father of a living son, and brushed away the tear. His father was crying, the image never left him in spite of the fact that even then the thought flashed out: "or maybe drooling."

 *XXI*

Karpstein felt his shirt getting clammy. In the darkness of a hidden corner of his hidden building he was seeing his long dead father.

Big Al turned and faced his living son. The long dead man held one hand to his face. A tear, the one that rolled down his cheek as he lay in a pine box in a funeral home many years before, was etched there in layers of dust. "You hit me," he said softly.

A tightness pulled a silent sob from deep in Theodore Karpstein's chest. He felt tears rush to his eyes. He reached a hand forward to touch that familiar, weathered face. But Big Al never seemed to be in range for his son to touch him—not then, not now.

"You hit me."

Karpstein had hit him. In fear, in frustrated desperation, in the middle of one stormy screaming match, Theodore—Teddy—Karpstein had raised his hand to ward off a threatened blow and slammed it into the startled face of Big Al. When flesh and flesh made contact the younger Karpstein had recoiled and cringed with more terror than he ever before had known. Armageddon, annihilation, apocalypse he had expected to rain down. Ancient taboos had been broken. A boundary had crumbled. Even an atheist could expect the wrath of God to flare to punish so heinous a crime. For an instant of terror, time stopped, but no hideous punishment came. Instead, the raging furrier stopped in mid sentence, turned and, like some wounded mammoth, walked away.

The incident marked some moment of forever change in the rhythm of their life and, less than one year later, when Big Al joined the deceased, all the many sorrys had still not been said.

"You hit me"

"I was frightened. You always were shouting."

"I wanted you to hear me—to learn things. I wanted to teach you so many things."

"I wanted to listen, but you shouted all the time. I'm sorry I hit you—so very sorry…"

"Teddy—you hit me—I loved you. I couldn't help shouting—I got excited—it's just my way. Maybe I should have said I love you."

From a shadowy corner of a shadowy building a mourning howl went up against the sky. Karpstein collapsed on heaps of disintegrating newspaper and lay unmoving except for the heaving rhythm of his sobs. Bitter dust clawed at his throat and his tears made gobs of mud on his yellowed pulp cushion. A low keening moan flowed from him—through him. He tried to sing the ancient prayer for the departed—V'yisgadol; v'yisgadas—but his mind and mouth would not bring forth the words and so he just poured out a wordless lament. In the darkened building his voice was just another instrument in a wind-whipped orchestra of undefinable sounds.

XXII

"I'm dying."

Karpstein thought he was dying. Fever warmed his small room and chilled it again. There was blood in his cough. The cough tore at him like knives. Karpstein coughed and cringed—terrified at the thought of being captured because of a cough. Nobody heard him.

The real world was very far away, but in his mind world they, the dangerous "they" who haunted Karpstein and defined his otherness, followed the sound to his hidden nest. For Karpstein, every rattle of a wind whipped window became a booted step on the stairs just below him and every wind roar was a voice urging the hunters forward.

Days and nights lost the seams that held them apart and together rolled past him like a solid sheet. The food supplies were almost gone but it didn't matter—Karpstein couldn't eat. The fever held on, unbreakable.

Mattress fever. Wall fever. Window fever. Sunlight fever. Moonlight fever. The bed roasted him. The ceiling spied on him. The walls laughed at him and threatened always to squeeze together and leave of him nothing more than an unseen stain in a room unremembered. Karpstein writhed.

"I'm dying and no one will know I even lived."

Then she came to help him.

He had awaited Death—imagining the traditional black hood, skull face, scythe and ancient sand-clock. But she was not death—she was only one of death's previous conquests. She was Kalila.

They had parted, Karpstein and his lover, Kalila, a name she had chosen obscurely, from a dream, she said. They had drifted together, floated together, drifted apart and then parted.

In a coffee house, in a long blur of coffee house evenings Karpstein met Kalila. She was sitting with his friend, Zalman Fleischkopf when Karpstein walked into the smoky cafe. Fleischkopf, was a poet whose major—and perhaps only—achievement was the publication of a slim volume about a highly romanticized working class that even the working class wouldn't recognize. The pudgy, pockmarked, scraggly-bearded poet had an uncanny success with women. Karpstein did alright on his own, but it always took some effort. Fleischkopf just seemed to gesture at his choices and they obediently followed him home.

"Kalila—Teddy Karpstein," was the full extent of Fleischkopf's inelegant introduction. "Sit down, Karpstein."

Karpstein sat down. He and the woman exchanged nods. She added a sad, almost shy, smile to hers. Karpstein tried to look away. This was probably another one of Zalman's muses. The word wordslinger always called them his muses and fell madly in love with them to the point of fiery, dangerous jealousy. He wrote mediocre verses to them and then walked away from them like strangers. Fleischkopf had once broken a bottle over the head of another writer who dared to buzz too close to a simpering muse named Rochelle. Two weeks later Fleischkopf and Karpstein were walking together when they saw Rochelle sitting in a small park. Fleischkopf turned abruptly and led them away from the park and back into the noisy city streets.

"It's over, he grunted in response to Karpstein's inquiry. "She bored me."

It was not difficult to see why his muses always bored him after a short fling. They were usually boring people. Kalila was an immediate exception. From her smile to her brown eyes, deep pools too bottomless to look into safely, Kalila was not boring.

She was also not one of Fleischkopf's muses.

After a while the poet excused himself, half heartedly invited them to come hear him read one of his lugubrious epics at another coffee house halfway across town and, after their polite refusals, left. Karpstein sat alone with Kalila and Kalila with him. They talked for a while and then, as if it were the most natural thing in the world, went home to Karpstein's apartment and became lovers.

* * *

Kalila was soft. Her body had roundnesses Karpstein found himself exploring again and again after the fire of their love-making had subsided. She was not the body on the pin-up calendars in the warehouse or the gym. Hers was a body that great sculptors and painters of other ages understood, but his own time had forgotten. Karpstein felt a glow of warmth and, he imagined, saw a glow of light around the soft curves of Kalila.

There was a fire to their lovemaking, but not an urgency. It started with a kiss that had surprised them both while they walked the silent blocks to Karpstein's lodgings. From there, there was touching. First-time touching without the awkwardness of first time. Such was the softness that radiated from Kalila and the gentleness that lay lightly sleeping inside Karpstein.

Her fingers pondered the newness of his taut-muscled body and the furry down of man hair that covered it. He held the fullness of her breasts as if discovering some never seen or tasted fruit. They wandered like curious deer over each other's meadows. Karpstein sent his hand exploring supple expanse of belly, around bulge of hips and onto warm and ample thighs. She swayed to the slow rhythm of his hands, rolling her body closer to his inquiring fingers. She made small, soft sounds of pleasure. Her hands flowed softly over his body as well. Again and again their lips met and darted tongues to rendezvous with each other. Then, timid hands growing slowly bolder, he sought the silky center of her. Heat and wetness greeted his fingers. His own heat intensified. His probing, gently stroking touch broke down the final, invisible barriers between them. Before they had been strangers. Now they were new friends sharing passion.

Kalila stroked and played with Karpstein's hardness. He was excited as seldom before. He held back and let himself recede down the peaks of rapture each time his body seemed ready to erupt. Then she said, "Enter me."

Karpstein pushed slowly into her. The warmth of their bodies melted into one warmth heated to boiling.

From that first intertwining they grew to be lovers in spirit and heart as well as flesh. For more than a year Karpstein and Kalila floated, soared and stormed together. Through volatile tempests of sex, thunderous battles of opinion, explosive departures and euphoric reunitings, they maintained an alliance that seemed inseparable. Inseparable even through the storms. Then, after one storm too many, it ended; they ended; she ended.

The ending storm—as all storms—grew from reason of no reason— from no real reason.

"What did you do that for?" (Distant thunder.)

"Why are you talking to me like that?" (Answering thunder.)

"Who the fuck do you think you are?" (Roar coming closer.)

"Well fuck you, asshole!" A pointing, jabbing, threatening finger dances out the stinging words. (Lightning joins the rumbling thunder.)

Crashing thunder, hurting whips of sound, the expected but unanticipated hiss of lightning hands darting with menacing gestures into neutral space.

"Oh yeah, then take your fucking, lousy clock."

This time they had started over a clock—CRRrrraaaaassssh—direct hit lightning bolt as clock flying faster than time ever flew meets standing still wall and falls, brokenfaced, on the floor.

"Well shove the clock up your ass. You broke the goddammed clock and now I'm leaving." (This storm had rain, too.)

Sometimes she left; sometimes he left. Until the end, neither stayed away. The return was always filled with remorse and a rebirth of tenderness.

"This love stuff, I never thought it was real. It seemed like so much bourgeois crap before we got together," Karpstein often told her.

"I never really believed that love was possible before this," Kalila would tell Karpstein.

Sometimes, when darkness or passion had weakened defenses or maybe wisdom, "I need you, I need you," is what one would tell the other.

The storms still came. Ugly anger and jagged words left scars even where the ensuing tenderness healed the wounds. But Kalila and Teddy still shared the same bed and read the same books.

The end still came. It ended; they ended; she ended; maybe from accident, maybe from illness or maybe from self. No matter, dead.

She was, they surmised, on a cliff by the sea.

Perhaps a fever made her faint over the edge. She had been ill that week.

Maybe a crumbling edge gave way and brought her down. Spring rainstorms had sent other chunks of earth and rock cascading down all around the place they assume she fell.

Perhaps she had tried to fly over a cliff and sail the thermals that gulls and ospreys traveled.

Or was it simply a parachute ride, freely taken, out of life?

Kalila's last moments were lost in the sea of conjecture. Kalila's body was lost in the sea of reality that grabbed it and played roughly with it for two days before tossing it on a beach where terrified children found it.

Now she, Kalila, just as soft and full as life, came to his hidden room. In the haze of the fever, he saw her hover near his bed. The vision of Kalila came at an hour when Karpstein had been awaiting Death. Karpstein, who had once declared Death just another visitor to be treated with open hospitality now asked the dead Kalila to bar the door.

"Don't let him come," Karpstein tried to make his voice sound authoritative as he pleaded with her. "You're nodding? Yes? You say you can protect me?"

Kalila hovered silently. Karpstein just waited. He wanted to ask Kalila the truth about her death, but he was afraid she would tell instead the truth about his own.

He tried to sleep, but the ache-provoking fever kept him restless in an uncomfortable world of wakefulness.

The water stained walls surrounding Karpstein faded away and dull blue walls took their place.

It was the hospital. Teddy Karpstein was six years old and his tonsils were about to leave him. The hospital was a frightening, foreign place. It was Sane John's hospital.

Teddy Karpstein didn't know who Sane John was or whether there was also a Crazy John. Maybe it was one and the same person. Maybe Crazy John had been carried away, screaming at people nobody else could see and throwing books out the window like his aunt Rachel had been. Maybe Crazy John had been carried to this very hospital and cured here and that's why it was named Sane John in his honor. Perhaps Sane John was the man in a bathrobe and nightgown carrying a big stick whose statue stood in front of the hospital and also in front of the Sane John school in Karpstein's neighborhood. Teddy Karpstein knew that crazy or sane, this man John had something to do with the goyim. He was one of their heroes. Possibly he was the one who told them to yell at Teddy and the other Jewish kids who passed by the school, to chase them and to throw things at them.

Karpstein imagined this man John, with his robe and stick, skulking through the semi-dark corridors of the hospital at night. What if he saw Teddy Karpstein there? And what if he found out he was Jewish? The thought made young Karpstein shiver with fear and promise himself he would fight away sleep.

He looked around the room at the other four beds. One was empty. Young boys close to his own age occupied the other three. One had plaster casts on both arms and one leg. His stark white limbs were attached to straps that held them upward to a frame over the bed. The boy, who a nurse said, had fallen or jumped out of a window, looked like a grotesque marionette waiting for a giant puppet master to animate him. His eyes were open but he didn't seem to see. Once in a while he moaned softly or whimpered. Later that night he would suddenly burst forth with wild, hysterical screams until a flurry of nurses came running to inject him with sleep again.

Also awake was the boy whose appendix had been taken by the same collectors who would soon add Karpstein's tonsils to their stockpile of defective body parts. He, his name was James, seemed to be taking it all as some great adventure. Teddy Karpstein envied him.

Next to Karpstein's bed was a normally talkative boy, now silent, whose eyes were bandaged over. One couldn't tell if he was awake or asleep, only that he was silent. During the day he sent his words out as a kind of radar, constantly asking for descriptions of every sound, of every action, of every person who entered or passed by in the corridor. When the food came he smelled and touched everything on the tray and made the assistant nurse who came to feed him recite the name and size and color of each thing before she lifted a fork to his lips. No one knew whether his darkness would be permanent, but he fought desperately to hold on to his memories of light.

Suddenly an unanticipated nun, all starchy white and black, swept into the ward. She carried what looked like a small baby bottle with a salt shaker cover instead of a nipple. She moved swiftly from bed to bed.

"Have you said your prayers tonight?"

"Yes, Sister."

Whoosh, a flick of the wrist and a light sprinkle from the bottle landed on the foot of the bed.

"Have you said your prayers tonight?"

"Yes, Sister."

(So the bandaged boy was awake after all.)

Whoosh.

"Have you said your prayers tonight?"

A whimper of assent from the broken puppet boy.

Whoosh.

Now it was Karpstein's turn. He felt a chill of dread. He was some kind of imposter here.

"Have you said your prayers tonight?"

In Karpstein's semi-atheistic house, prayer was a fairly alien concept. He had heard of it, but always assumed it was some strange ritual performed only by goyim. He never equated the melodic *davenning*, the rocking back and forth while chanting Hebrew words, that he had seen on infrequent synagogue visits, with anything called "prayer."

"But I'm Jewish," he told the harsh looking apparition.

She paused, her automated rhythm of bed visits broken, and curled her upper lip in disgust.

"Well, you must pray to *something*," she hissed at him. She hesitated, glaring at him, and then shook her baby bottle in his direction. A minishower of clear droplets hit his hospital blanket. Karpstein had heard some Catholic kids at school talk about "holy water" and he guessed that this was it. Then she spun and swept out the door.

Karpstein lay there, afraid to move. What kind of substance was this holy water that had been sprinkled on him? The first time he had heard the phrase his young mind wondered how water could have holes in it. What would it do to him? He also pictured the woman in the starched costume running to spread the alarm that a Jew was lying in Mr. Sane John's hospital.

He hadn't asked to be there and he didn't like being there. He would rather live with the frequent soreness and coughs and colds difficult swallowing that some unseen creatures in his throat seemed to attract. Sickness at home was better than sickness in this unfamiliar place of sickness. His parents told him he was here because it was the nearest hospital to their house that was covered by his father's union's insurance plan. Teddy's parents had delivered him into the hands of the enemy and left him there, vulnerable and alone. He pulled the sheet over his face and began to cry.

Karpstein woke up crying, but he was a different Karpstein and this was a different aloneness. The old and cracking walls of his tower were back. He looked around for Kalila, but she had left for good. He felt weak, but clearer. The burning in his head was gone. He had survived his affliction.

XXIII

The food was gone.

Once the illness passed, the appetite came back. There was no foraged feast to welcome it home. The last crumbs had been hunted down and swallowed, but that only made hunger pangs worse. It was time to scavenge. Karpstein decided to leave the building by climbing down the stairs. He was too dizzy to risk the secret route of pipes and tunnels. Karpstein seldom used the stairs when he left his building. The last part of the stair journey led right past the office where the watchman spent his solitary nights.

Karpstein tucked his food sack into his jacket and undid the trap-door ladder. Every effort was magnified. He was sweating and panting even before his feet touched the floor of the corridor below his hiding place. He let the ladder swing upward again and pull the door closed. This time he didn't drag the red chair with him or leave the rope hanging. As weak as he was, he'd have to dare the tubes and tunnels of his secret entrance on the return trip. Entering the building any other way presented too much danger of discovery.

The stairway was long and dusty and, as he neared the ground floor, Karpstein forced himself to suppress dangerous coughs more than once. A few times he was startled by the sudden scurrying of rats or mice that gathered around crusts and sandwich scraps discarded by warehouse workers. If only his own food hunting were that easy.

Between the third and second floors Karpstein found a sign that work and lunch were not the only concerns of his building's daytime inhabitants. Lying on a landing, glistening in the light of one of the few functioning 40-watt bulbs, was a used condom.

"Coney Island jellyfish," he thought. The term was one he hadn't thought of since his childhood. These white fishes floated near the shore not only at Coney Island, but at every beach where the Karpsteins swam. He almost laughed aloud and then had to work even harder to stifle a cough.

On the ground floor the stairway ended at a fire door permanently propped open in violation of both safety laws and common sense. There was a dangerous stretch of open space in front of the watchman's doorless office. Just beyond that four more steps led to a locked exit door. To the right of that another flight of steps—eleven to be exact—headed into the first level of the basement. That was Karpstein's destination.

At the bottom of the main stairway Karpstein stopped and listened. He didn't hear the watchman stirring. Perhaps he was out on his rounds. Karpstein waited. Then he heard a light and rhythmic snoring. The building's nighttime protector was asleep. Karpstein got down on hands and knees and crawled. Karpstein knew the office well. It had been the timekeeper's station when Karpstein worked in the building. A narrow counter stood between the desk where the watchman dozed and the hallway. Once past the door Karpstein could stand again and tiptoe down the steps. The exit door was out of the question. Even if it weren't locked, opening it set off an insistent bell. The alarm was not so much for safety as it was to prevent workers from sneaking out early. The final steps to the basement were relatively easy to maneuver even in the dark.

Karpstein felt a rush of giddy dizziness, partly from the exertion of the journey thus far and partly from his relief at having made it this far safely. He leaned against a damp wall and caught his breath. Ahead of him a sliver of light marked his destination. The light came from a streetlamp shining into a sidewalk grating. The window was often propped open to ventilate the small workspace in that corner of the basement. If the window was closed, as it was this time, it could be pried up easily. Karpstein climbed onto a workbench and eased his way out the window. The grating above him made him feel like he was in a cage. For a moment he relished the feeling. A cage at least was a safe place—and caged things were fed.

Karpstein had used this exit before. He knew exactly where to push to get the cold metal grate to move. In a few seconds he was on the street. Except for the sounds of distant traffic, the night was still. Karpstein looked at the sky. Milky clouds covered the moon and the stars. He had no way of knowing the time, but his instincts usually guided him. He would make his rounds and then crawl back into his nest before the morning people took over the rest of his building.

The breeze chilled Karpstein's sweaty body, reviving him and sapping him simultaneously. The paths were familiar, but Karpstein found his own steps strange and hollow as he pursued his own shadow toward the remembered sources of food.

A bin behind a supermarket yielded edible scraps including a smashed package of sweet buns Karpstein tore apart and ate with shaking hands. All the while his vigilance never faded. Every sound

made him jump. He crouched and hid and listened. There were no chal-
lengers to his hunt. Soon the delivery trucks would roll and Karpstein
would follow in their wake collecting sustenance like some ghostly bird
behind a fishing boat.

Crates awaited him at the alley side door of a produce and grocery
store named Sung's Food Center. Karpstein had seen a dead man in this
alley once; a glassy eyed corpse with a needle hanging impotently from
a scabby arm. This was the first time he returned since that terrifying
meeting almost a year before. Now his fear of being caught was
magnified by the haunted fear of memory.

The largest crate held oranges. Survival food. Karpstein remembered
horror stories in school about sailors who died toothless deaths of
scurvy for the want of a citrus fruit. He pried up the top of the crate and
began his harvest.

"Alright!"

Ice ran through Karpstein. He couldn't run. He had been careless and
now he was found. He turned with arms raised to ward off a blow.

"It's OK, man. I ain't out for no bad."

Karpstein's heart raced. He felt like a puppet whose strings had just
been cut. He couldn't move or speak. He just dangled. The icy sensation
in his body turned to waves of weakness and he fought with his legs not
to cave in. The speaker, moving now from the invisibility of pre-dawn
shadows to the streetlight streaked alley, was a thin black man wearing
a wrinkled and dirty, maroon suit and a burgundy fedora that had, like
its wearer, seen better days.

He came closer. "I ain't making no trouble. Just looking for food, just
like you. Now you got it open, let me take from it too."

Karpstein found his tongue. "Only a few from the top."

Terror still gripped him. Being seen in his food gathering rounds was
one of his biggest fears and now it had happened, but all the stranger
wanted was food and Karpstein couldn't deny him.

"After we take we close it up and shake it so they won't see any missing," Karpstein explained. "Otherwise they might stop leaving it here."

Karpstein's apprehension subsided. The stranger was not attacking him or calling for the stormtroopers, so further explanation was not needed. The important business of gathering sustenance had to continue before time ran out. With Karpstein as guide the two scurried from place to place snatching up bits of food to carry away. Karpstein did his sneaking, crouched run up an alley or across a deserted street and the newcomer, who said his name was Carver, followed him.

"You good at this," Carver told Karpstein. "You been on the streets a long time."

Karpstein's too well worn clothing had a comfortableness to it. Carver's improbable suit was new but old. It was outdated, but it had been used only a short time. It looked like it came from a box on a long-forgotten shelf and Carver had recently started wearing it to sleep in. The almost matching hat looked no better. It was the same not old, not new mystery as the suit. The shoes were not part of the puzzle. They were unmistakably shabby. The thin black man in the maroon suit was also old and new. White hair framed his lined face and his movement was spry rather than agile, but there was an awkwardness of unfamiliarity to his actions. He seemed, like his suit, unused but wrinkled.

With Carver a few paces at his heels the dangerous journey seemed even more chancy. It certainly was slower. Time was not on their side. Once they had to hide in a hallway for almost ten minutes while an early crew of trash collectors worked a nearby alley.

"Someone after you?" Carver, frozen like a statue next to statue Karpstein in the hallway, asked out of almost unmoving lips.

"Yes, many."

When they went on their way the street was awakening. The sounds of motors and machines echoed from the distance. Twice they had to drop to the ground behind garbage cans and dumpsters as dawn shift workers trudged past them. The expedition had been started too late and the slowness of his weakened condition had let him drift into that dangerous, city waking time of pink spreading night end. Karpstein panicked.

"How will I get back? They'll see me!"

He was ready to drop his almost full sack of food and run back to his hidden shelter. He had no food there, but what good was food when you were dead? Carver saw his agitation. "Where do you stay? Maybe you can still make it."

"No, it's too late. The first workers come at 6:30. They'll see me." He started to sob. Carver put a hand on Karpstein's arm.

"We near my place. You can stay there now. Nobody will see you."

Karpstein stared into the unfamiliar dark brown face. He was being asked to trust the man who wore it. The eyes, like the eyes showing through a mask, were far away and seemed to belong to another, distant and unshown, face. There was no choice.

"Where," he rasped.

"Follow," was the reply.

Now Karpstein was the guided, scurrying worriedly behind Carver of the maroon red suit.

Karpstein's mind raced wildly. This man, he thought, must also be in hiding. He expected a tunnel like his home tunnels, closets long sealed, caves, sewers of a romantic Paris never seen. Instead they ran up seven wide, stone steps and entered the ordinary hallway of a dilapidated apartment house. At the end of the hallway they went down a dozen steps into a cellar that smelled of mildew. The surface under their feet was wet earth. Broken furniture and rotting mattresses, hulking shapes in the semi-darkness, formed an apathetic gauntlet through which they zigzagged with their sacks of food.

Karpstein helped Carver move a mattress that sagged innocently against one wall. Behind it was a door made of thick planks. Carver had a key on a string around his neck and pulled it forth from under his shirt. He unlocked a large padlock and pulled open the door. It was a storage area that had been transformed into a room. Carver pulled the door shut behind them and drew a heavy iron bolt into place. The chamber had some of the same austerity as Karpstein's own quarters. A cot-like single bed took the wall with the small, barred window that looked out at ground level into the littered back yard, and a tired sofa took the other wall. A small, wooden crate, turned upside down served as a low table. The bed was made neatly with its tattered, woolen blanket pulled and tucked taut. A pair of scuffed, but still glossy in places, patent leather shoes stood precisely heel to heel and toe to toe next to each other under the bed. Everything in the apartment looked like it had been laid out with a T-square and then put in place. Dishes—two tin plates, two chipped mugs, two bowls, and a matching amount of mismatched silverware, were all stacked neatly on a counter next to a stained washbasin. A bandaged garden hose entering like a snake through a floor level hole in the wall was obviously the only source of water. A salt shaker, a pepper shaker and diner style sugar pourer were lined up in a fastidious row on the windowsill. The only decorations were two color photos—one of an idyllic cottage in the woods and the other of an aerial view of a block of city houses—both torn from magazines and glued directly to the wall.

"This is my place. You can stay here. They won't nobody find you here."

Karpstein was numb with a strange mixture of fear and gratitude. His thankfulness was not so much to Carver as it was to Karpstein's own vague notion of God. He often mouthed the name of God in his panics—"God please help me. Please God, don't let them find me…" It was the same way he might have screamed for Mama when he was younger. It was seldom that he actually connected his moments of survival or sustenance to any particular source when his pleas for rescue were no longer needed. Suddenly, in the house of this equally lost stranger, Karpstein felt appreciation.

⸎ *XXIV*

In the morning they sat quiet; sitting on quiet in a quiet room, looking at quiet, listening to the unquiet quiet of the streets somewhere outside and slightly above them. In the afternoon they played checkers.

"Play checkers?"

Karpstein reached for his voice and found a raspy whisper, "OK, sure."

Carver reached for a square, flat cardboard candy box from one of his tidy shelves. He slid a chair between the two bunks and set the box down on it. Inside the box lid was a hand-drawn checkerboard. The squares were either yellow, the color of the box lid, or black crayon rubbed on over the yellow. The checkers were also crayoned card-board—red-orange and black.

"I brought it with me when I left," Carver nodded toward the checkers set.

"Left?"

"I was away—for long time."

"Away." Karpstein paused and thought about that. He too had been away for a while. "Were you hiding?"

"I hid at first—at my brother's house—but they find me."

"They found you?"

"Somebody squealed—we think it was the neighbor."

"And they caught you?"

"Yeah. Double jump." Two of Karpstein's checkers fell captive to Carver's onslaught.

"Oh. And your brother?"

"They didn't want him. They just want me."

"But they let you live?"

"My lawyer make them let me live. In the beginning I think I rather die. Then I think maybe I do die. Plenty damn dangerous up there."

"Lawyer? You had a lawyer?" For Karpstein, all laws had ceased. If he were caught there would be no lawyer, no jury.

"Court give me a lawyer."

"And he kept them from killing you?"

"She."

"She?"

"She. The lawyer was a she. Mrs. Cohen—a Jewish lady."

"And she kept them from killing you?"

"I'm here ain't I? They give me life."

"Life?"

"But I get out. They let me go after 27 years. That was 51 days ago. They give me nothing but the suit I was wearing when I went in—they had it in a locker somewhere all wrinkled up—and my shoes—and a letter supposed to help me find a job."

The outburst of conversation exhausted both men. They maneuvered their cardboard checkers in silence for a while. Finally the question that was almost asking itself sprang out of Karpstein's lips almost without any action on his part.

"What was it?"

Carver's answer, waiting on the end of his tongue like spittle, came out with equal ease.

"I killed two guys."

∞ *XXV*

This man who killed men didn't frighten Karpstein. Karpstein had seen death, had dreamed death, had smelled death all around him. "Who after you?" Carver asked him, quite simply.

"I am a Jew."

"And I am a black man. Who chasing you?"

"It's the pogroms."

"Pogroms, what's that?"

"They are beating and killing my people in the streets."

"Mine too."

"It has spread," Karpstein whispered in shocked sadness.

"More in some places than others."

"How many dead?" Karpstein who hid from news wanted to know the day's news or the week's or at most the month's. How many dead? Was it growing or waning? Would it ever be safe to come out of hiding?

Carver, whose news consisted of two histories—the history of his own beaten life and the history of his people which he learned while in prison—told the century's news. "Thousands dead. Lynched dead, beaten dead, electrocuted dead like they would have done me and gas chamber dead."

Gas chambers. So the pogroms had increased. Karpstein saw gas chambers in his dreams. Relatives he never could have known had died in gas chambers he had never seen. The scourge had spread. How long could he hide?

Carver's tales of black pogrom deaths intertwined in Karpstein's mind with the Jew pogrom he was rat hole hiding from. The story, the narration, the gushing, sometimes spurting chant of deaths and dying dispensed freely by the very gentle handed Carver surrounded Karpstein. The swirling images of death, the tales of pain, the frustration of injustice all blended with and reinforced Karpstein's own inner dialogues of destruction.

Carver told of prisoners crying and puking and freaking out with hysterical chattering of life stories, of innocence, of prayers, of baby prayers sometimes given in a baby talk voice as a condemned convict regressed on the way back toward the earth. There were orgiastically detailed accounts of prisoners strapped in to the "uncomfortable chair" and getting zapped. Carver was 51 days old in the world. This was the first real talking he had done since his release and once begun it was a hard flow to staunch. Karpstein had talked during his exile, but only to ghosts. There was much he needed to ask.

"But they're still killing Jews?" Karpstein wanted to know.

"Oh, yeah, I guess there was some Jews," Came Carver's answer, missing the question by just a short distance.

❧ *XXVI*

There was fitful talking, sharing of food, fitful sleeping, waiting. Sounds of the world seeped in but the world did not intrude on the secrecy of their hiding and their sharing. Day passed and darkness returned to the streets.

"I've got to go," Karpstein told his host.

"Got to get back to your hideout."

"Thank you, Carver."

"No thanks needed. I just hope they never ever find you."

"Your name will be written in the book of good deeds."

"I don't expect so. Good luck man."

Karpstein threw his arms stiffly around the other man's shoulders in a perfunctory embrace.

"You all knows where I stay, man. Drop around and visit my cell again sometime," Carver told Karpstein as the latter headed toward the uncertain street and his circuitous journey to the secret tubes and tunnels of his own hidden cell.

Karpstein imagined invisibility and tried to see all in his path. He hated the unexpected. Karpstein was the unexpected. He was the unanticipated guest, hidden in a corner where nobody was searching. He was a surprise, but, as he darted from shadow to shadow in his covert journey homeward he had no desire to encounter other surprises.

When the woman spoke to him, he hissed. He took an abrupt inward breath and his air rushing through clenched teeth was as raw-edged a hiss as any adder emitted. The woman in the shadows was a shadow, she was a surprise. For Karpstein surprises were all flavored with danger. In his mind the sound of marching boots kept coming closer. In his mind the sound of shattering glass, of screaming, of dying, all drew closer. He was a fugitive from those sounds, from his mind.

Unexpected dangers brought the terrors closer. In Karpstein's tangled mesh of fear and memory, surprises brought the threat of capture and death ever closer.

"Do you want a date?" The voice was raspy and weathered, but it was a woman's voice. "Do you want me, honey?"

Karpstein flattened against a wall and stared into the dimness. He had just scampered across an unavoidable pool of streetlight and plunged into what he thought was the safety of a dark side street. It was past midnight. He thought he would be alone in the darkness. He squinted toward the silhouettes to see what phantasm owned the voice. He half imagined some cauldron-stirring wraith like the mist-shrouded crones who accosted MacBeth. Shapes emerged from the obscurity as his eyes regained their balance with the dark and he saw the woman. She was young and old at once. Now he could see her clearly. A knitted dress hugged the curves and draped around the sunken hollows of her unnaturally thin body. Dark hair hung straight down around her gaunt face. The whiteness of her skin seemed to glow in contrast to the darkness of the street.

The woman saw Karpstein too. She sized him up and realized that this potential John probably had no money and therefore no potential at all. She stopped trying to push her shrunken breasts against the tightness of the dress and slumped against the wall.

"It's alright, honey, I can see you're broke. You got a cigarette? I'm dying for a fucking cigarette."

Karpstein's sudden rush of anxiety released him long enough for him to stammer that he didn't. Karpstein didn't smoke. He had never smoked.

"It's OK, it's OK," she told him. "Don't be so afraid, I don't bite. I was just hoping to find one last trick to make my day."

"I don't have any money," he confessed, as if that were some dark secret not broadcast by his threadbare clothes and shabby shoes.

"Yeah, I see that. But you're cute, I like you, do you want to fuck me anyway?"

The words exploded for Karpstein like carelessly flicked water landing in a frying pan of sizzling oil. He recoiled and gasped.

"Hey, I ain't that bad looking am I," she demanded. The grating voice cracked for a moment. Karpstein's reaction had stimulated the same dismay in her as her words had in him. She quickly festered toward anger. "What's the matter don't you like me? Don't you like girls?"

Karpstein could only mumble conciliatory replies. He wanted to run from the place and seek the familiar safety of his private cell, but he felt rooted to the site. He was fascinated by the woman. She was the first living woman he had spoken to in all of his exile. He inhaled her. There was an edge of alcohol and the acrid odors of the street curling around her, but the dominating smell—the one that hypnotized him—was her perfume. It was some ordinary, dime-store smelly water, but to

Karpstein's starved senses it could have been the official harem fragrances of Araby.

She was shouting. "What the fuck's the matter with you, you asshole? I was offering you a free fuck. Don't you flinch away from me! There are plenty of guys who would pay plenty to touch me."

Surprises meant danger, shouting meant far greater danger. Soon people would come. In Karpstein's world of hiding, being seen denoted getting caught. He must get away and merge with the darkness again. But the woman held him spellbound. He had not been with a woman in so long. While one inner voice screamed for him to leave, another negotiated possibilities. He could go with her—NO! He could take her with him—NO! He could arrange to meet her somewhere—NO! He could risk it all and fall panting and groaning with her in the darkness of an alley with his body's howl for satisfaction transcending all the warning signs of danger—NO NO NO!

Somewhere above, a light went on and a window scraped open. "Shut up ya lousy whore or I'll call the cops," a voice threatened.

Karpstein ran; not the shadow-hugging scuttling of a hidden creature, but a full terror dash that did not stop until he fell winded in a familiar alley near his warehouse fortress.

"I like you, I do like you. I was afraid," he told the darkness. He thought he could still smell and taste the sickly sweet waves of her perfume ocean.

❧ *XXVII*

Karpstein fell. Karpstein fell miles without landing. Karpstein woke up
sweating, gripping the edges of his mattress in the most private room of
his secret hotel of memories. Karpstein fell in dreams when the three
hundred and six metal rungs of his ladder into the sanctuary all turned
to rubber and betrayed his searching feet. Karpstein fell when he stood
on a cliff where a long dead lover had chosen to join the sea and lost his
balance while glancing for a distracted moment at improbable women
walking below. He fell when familiar doors opened suddenly to reveal
expected abysses. He tumbled downward when corridors vanished and
gaping space awaiting him instead. Karpstein plunged and woke up
whimpering alone with no one to hear him or help him. He plummeted

alone with no one to come and tell him his waiting monster-in-the-closet was not really there.

Karpstein also flew. He stepped out on air and gravity no longer owned him. He catapulted into endless air and looked down from bird height. His spread arms embraced clouds. Karpstein glided above danger. Earth concerns were no longer his. Karpstein looked up and stretched and soared above roomfuls and streets full of people who reached up to grasp him, to torment him or to touch him.

The flying Karpstein awakened in a tangle of ragged bedding, his body and mind aroused, his erection pushing against his shabby blankets.

∞ *XXVIII*

Boredom. It was a journey of boredom in a night of boredom. Karpstein sat in his hiding cave listening to the sounds of the night and feeling the coldness of the night. He had food. The hunger was not in his stomach, but he felt hunger. His room hugged him and confined him. He was protected there and smothered there. In his room nobody could touch him. In his room he could touch nobody.

The objects in Karpstein's room, like the objects in the room of Mr. Carver who had spent a lifetime in prison cells, were stacked and lined up and folded arranged and dusted and lined up again. The result, in Karpstein's room, was not the same neat precision found in Carver's room. The extra blankets were never folded quite square, the kitchen utensils never lined up quite straight.

The books stood in a sagging, unruly row against one wall. The odd assortment of randomly scavenged books—from Buber and Camus to the punch-in-the-mouth, hard-riding boilerplate of the detective novels and westerns—had compressed some of the hours, but neither they nor anything else could lift him from this boredom in which Karpstein now wallowed.

The room was a cell, but Karpstein was free to wander and explore. He could walk out of the tight square of safety above the tower before the square grew even smaller. He untied the rope and pried loose the wooden bar that held his ladder and trapdoor in place.

Karpstein prowled. The rooms filled with lives sometimes broke boredom with their surprises. He found new worlds when he explored his castle.

He had seen rooms that had been ransacked. A nephew or a daughter or a grandchild with a need could always talk or lie or steal to conjure a key. Like vultures they came to look at and strip the few valuable crumbs from the trunks and boxes. The rooms filled with junk were still fantasized by some as sources of treasures unknown. The thefts were reported only rarely. Even then, they were not given much thought, by the storage company, by the watchman, or by the police the one or two times they were called. These redistributions of almost forgotten belongings were, it seemed, considered real events only by the renters who complained about them.

Karpstein saw a room down on the sixth floor with its padlock hanging open on its hasp, its door gaping. He stood listening. He approached with the wariness of a food foraging street shadow who knew in his mind that continued life depended on stealth. He concluded he was alone there. He was right, the marauding visitor was long gone. The trunks were open and raked through. Boxes were cut open and sifted. Remainders were strewn on the floor. The few odds and ends carried away had probably been sold already, or traded. There were no books there.

Then in a corner he saw a bicycle. It was a small bike, a green and blue bike, his bike or a bike so much like his many years ago bicycle.

Young Karpstein had wanted, so deeply wanted, had longed for, had craved a bike. A bicycle was movement. A bicycle was soaring away from the shouting that drowned all other sounds in his house. Karpstein's lusted after bicycle was another "we can't afford it" in a list of "we can't afford its" that covered the walls and the floors and the air and his skin for all the remembered years he lived at home.

But then there was a miracle. On a birthday—maybe twelfth, maybe fourteenth—he knew it was not the year of controversy of his Bar Mitzvah—a bicycle appeared. *For unto us a bicycle is born; unto us a bicycle is given.*

A magic bicycle. A green and blue bicycle with a loud bell. Teddy never really knew the full story of the bicycle. His parents gave it to him. His father, always impatient, always critical, taught him to ride it. But it was not really from them. Someone else(an uncle? a comrade?)gave money toward the magic bicycle. Teddy knew there was some barely hidden conflict about the bicycle, but at least he had it—for a while.

Karpstein touched the real bicycle and his memory bicycle was there. The bike had been given, but the bike was always about to be taken away. He touched the memory bicycle and heard his father's voice, "Put that damned thing somewhere else. If you keep leaving it in the way, I'll throw it right in the trash." And his mother, "If you don't clean up your room, you can kiss that bike goodbye." Even after the bike was his, it was not really his. Even after they bought it and gave it, they still argued and fought over it. But for Teddy, it was still magic. It carried him, at the speed of the wind that licked his face, away from the sound of their fighting and away from the pain of the shouting. When Teddy rode his green and blue bicycle he was the wind, he was flying, he was free. Then, while he was flying, the pedal had broken. The magic could not protect the metal and the metal had snapped. Once again, the magic bike went onto the list of "we can't afford its." Big Al promised to buy the part and to fix it, but the green and blue bike stood and was buried under a pile of promises that grew deeper and deeper.

Karpstein looked in the ransacked room at the dusty bicycle that leaned against a wall. He kicked it and it fell. One wheel spun slowly. "Why didn't you ever fix it?" he shouted. He stamped on the spinning wheel and felt spokes bend and break under his foot.

"Why did you give it to me if you didn't really want me to have it?" He kicked and stamped and smashed in fury until the small bike was as twisted and dented as he could cause it to be. He shouted and cursed until the flames of a more than forty year old pain were once again no more than embers. Then he walked. He walked the halls of silence and saw no more treasures. He moved from floor to floor and section to section like a shadow. He felt his aloneness. He saw no faces. He met no long dead family or friends. He heard only silence. His furtiveness and caution were eaten by his sorrow. That is how the watchman was able to find him. Karpstein rounded a corner and a man with a flashlight sprung back with fright. For each of them it was the materialization of that which they had avoided for so long. The watchman walked his rounds rarely. When he did it was more for exercise than with the expectation of finding an intruder. Who would seek to enter this dusty repository of mostly abandoned belongings? Karpstein had seen this man in dark corridors, but had always eluded him with ease. Now they confronted each other.

"What are you doing here?"

"I am here."

"I know you are here, I see you. But what are you doing here?"

"I live here."

"You live here?"

"Yes, I am hiding."

"What are you hiding from?"

"Why do you ask?"

"Who are your hunters?"

"Who have they always been?"

"Why won't you answer?"

"Am I not responding?"

"Who are you?"

Karpstein's heart was racing. He was afraid, but not in terror. Here was his greatest fear—discovery—and he felt surprisingly calm. He could run and hide in the passageways and rooms, but they would come with dogs and find him. In some ways he felt relief that it was over.

"Who are you?"

"Karpstein."

There was a long silence. The watchman looked at his strange visitor.

"Ok, let me get this straight. Your name is Karpstein?"

"Yes."

"And you live up here?"

"Yes."

"Why?"

"Why not?"

"Look, don't go starting that answering questions with questions routine again. You sound like my grandfather from Poland."

"Where in Poland?"

"Near... Hey, I'm supposed to ask the questions here."

"But where in Poland?"

"Near Vilna."

"You Jewish?"

"Yes, I'm Jewish. Barmitzvahed and the whole 9 yards, but that doesn't tell me what you're doing in this building. What do you mean you live here?"

"Are you safe?"

"What do you mean am I safe?"

"Do you feel safe?"

"Of course I feel safe."

"As a Jew?"

"Of course I…well, most of the time…"

"But they are rounding us up."

"They are?"

"To concentration camps and ovens."

"I read about that."

"You have not seen it?"

"It was a long time ago—before I was born."

"It's happening again. They're doing it now!"

Karpstein became more and more agitated as he spoke.

The guardian angel of the building where Karpstein lived had no desire to deal with an agitated man. He had taken this job because it gave the opportunity for a few hours of paid tranquility each day. On the two occasions when someone had attempted to break into the warehouse, he had hidden in a neutral corner and called the police. He was not armed.

"They're doing it again? Where?"

"Right here—Out in the streets. Is it not true?"

The younger man stared at Karpstein.

"It's true," he said cautiously. "It's true. Everything you say is true."

"You won't make me leave then?"

"You don't steal things, do you?"

"I am a Jew, not a thief," Karpstein answered emphatically.

"How long have you been here?"

"It is more than a year. I'm not sure. The *pogromchiks* tried to kill me, but I know how to hide from them."

"How long will you stay?"

"Until it is over."

"I won't send you away. I won't say that I saw you. Perhaps you don't even exist. Maybe you are just a dream."

"Perhaps I am—and you too. There are so many dreams in here."

The watchman turned and walked towards the elevator. He stopped and gestured toward Karpstein.

"Go hide. Go hide from your *pogromchiks* and your dreams. But don't let me find you again and don't steal anything. I don't need any trouble."

 *XXIX*

To a room in a place where Karpstein lived, a confusing uncle came with a woman sometimes called wife, sometimes called friend, sometimes called aunt. Uncle Chaim— "That means 'life' in Hebrew," he used to say again and again with a wink. Aunt Miriam. They came by surprise by way of Israel, of Argentina, of Poland, of many stories along the way with new names popping up in every retelling.

They came by surprise to a family who didn't seem to remember them except for Aunt Goldy who cried and cried and touched Uncle Chaim's face and called him Shmuel or Samuel and said over and over, "I thought you were dead. We heard you were shot."

From his Zaida, Karpstein heard tales of Jew hunters with clubs and sabers. From Shmuel-from-Lodz whose new name was Chaim, Karpstein learned about Jew hunters with high black boots and steel helmets. Chaim and Miriam were survivors. Both of them had numbers from the camps. Miriam's blue numbers, according to teenaged Karpstein, looked smooth and elegant against the creamy whiteness of her arm. Chaim's tough and hairy arms gave the tattooed numerals a coarse and chiseled look. Miriam and Chaim had met in the camps. Had lost each other. Had given each other up for dead. Had met again, by accident, in Israel. Had stayed together. Had lied and schemed their way to America on their way to some somewhere else.

"Yes I was shot. A bullet goes in and a bullet comes out the other side. But I didn't die. I just hid for a few months."

Karpstein, hidden for longer, saw in a familiar long corridor stories told by Shmuel Chaim and Aunt Miriam. In Karpstein's rooms the tales of running, of being caught, the camps, the camps, the camps lived again.

Familiar long corridor; ninth floor. Between two wings of the building was a long corridor with doors on both sides. Karpstein had been there many times. Now the corridor was filled with people. This was the street of the town of memory. Sounds, whispers, signs, the business of the day.

Booths, businesses, open air stalls lined corridor of street where Karpstein walked. In his head whispered a word, a name, a sound these people around him didn't know but he had learned from the stories that lived here again: Holocaust. Hollow Cast. How Low Cost. Such a juicy word to throw off walls and hear again if you were too young to know how much pain and shock was building up. In Karpstein's rooms he saw the newsreel films he had seen with every movie when he was young; newsreels of living dead in striped pajamas, of piles as big as houses of broomstick people lying very still. But here it was no newsreel Karpstein saw and walked in. He had seen the camps and camps and camps and he had been on the trains. Narrow corridors swaying, jolting, packed with stinking people dying or riding toward death.

Now he was in a bustling street, just like other streets the stories had shown him. Karpstein knew the capture was coming soon. Not his capture, he was one of the ones who ran and hid. Soon marching boots stilled other sounds until a piercing, cruel whistle sounded and the simmering of everyday chaos shattered into the seething of the chaos of hell.

He had seen what Shmuel Chaim and Miriam lived to run from. Hell, chaos, roundups in public squares, resisters shot in front of family and friends, families split and sent without warning to separate worlds, the rapes, the children killed, the madness. He had seen it before on other streets in his walls of memory.

Karpstein shifted, ill at ease, as the scene seemed ready to replay. He did not want to be there. Here there was terror. His heart pounded its urgent rhythm in quick time. He held his breath. The whistle came. But this time it was a ringmaster's whistle and a sour, funereal band began to play.

Instead of the hectic running (If you're surrounded where do you run?); instead of the crazed snatching at worthless goods to carry away (What do you take with you on a trip to hell?); instead of all the screaming madness was balletic slow motion. The players all wore makeup and floated, one leaping step at a time, through the space. Some juggled dishes or balanced pots. A man slow ran past carrying a small cow the size of a cat. A bearded, fur-hatted man with merry eyes danced away with a Torah the size of a wagon.

Karpstein floated with the honey slowness of the vision. The holocaust was turning into a circus for him. It was a distorted circus of strange apparitions. Two clowns loped toward him; one swatting the other with a large limp, doll. When they passed him he saw it was a bloodied baby. The tramp, tramp, tramp, tramp of a patrol is heard, but it is only soldierless boots—twelve pairs of black, shiny boots—in perfect cadence marching.

The band groaned on in discord; the offtune circus music making a somber mood.

For a finale, the entire stage roared with flames and entire families walked tightwires through the fires. Karpstein opened one of the doors and stepped into a room. It was cool and dark. Enough light came from a small, barred window to see the stacks and stacks of wooden shelves where people had slept. Nobody was there, but the place still hummed death marches inside its walls. Karpstein lay down on one of the benches and slept.

XXX

Outside, in the time before his internal banishment, Karpstein had never given much thought to the comings and departings of his people's holy days. They were markers to be taken for granted. Now the cycle of holidays helped him keep a frame around the seasons and the year so they didn't explode apart like a dropped vase and leave him sitting stunned among the shattered shards of days. Chanukah meant winter. Yom Kippur, the day of atonement announced the tangy fall. Today was *erev Pesach*, the eve of the holiday of Passover. Passover was a time for greeting the spring, a time for housecleaning, a time for remembering an exile in Egypt and slavery in all times.

Karpstein rearranged his few books and carefully brushed the dust from them. He stitched up a small rip in his ragged bed linen. The utensils were all wiped clean and stacked first one way and then another. Sunlight, a rare visitor in his hidden tower, reached through the dirt-smeared panel of the transom-sized skylight and leaned hard against the opposite wall. Karpstein didn't try to make clear and cogent pictures from the shimmering puddles of color dancing inside his brain.

In his sun-drenched cell Karpstein danced. He moved around his piles of possessions and touched each one, rearranging this pile, taking clothing or pieces of cloth from that one and shaking them out silently. There was no leavened bread in Karpstein's house, there were only fruits and vegetables. Even so, he searched the cracks and corners for forgotten crumbs the way he remembered his Bubbe doing. For the eight days of Passover there must be no trace of leavened bread in his possession. He could not replace it with matzoh, so he would go without bread altogether. In his exile, the rituals of exile were not possible. He could not recreate the joyous and elaborate seders he remembered from his Bubbe and Zaida's house, but he would hold a Passover celebration in his own way.

There was no wine for the blessings or to invite the presence of the ancient Prophet, Elijah, but Karpstein awaited his presence anyway. Karpstein would sing the *kiddush* blessing without wine. He would tell the story of exile, as commanded, but he would tell it to himself. He would, as the youngest one present, ask himself the four questions. "Why is this night different from all the nights in the year? *Mahnishtanah h'layleh hazeh...?* Why the unleavened bread of affliction? Why the bitter herb of affliction? Why the affliction? Why why why?" And as the oldest one present he would answer. "Because because because. Because we were strangers in a strange land."

Karpstein danced. He cleaned his world and he danced.

It was a Sunday. His building was quiet. Karpstein and the sunlight were there together. It was time for a walk. Creaking ladder. Red chair. Melancholy hallways brightened for a moment by Karpstein's dance. To the seventh room on the seventh floor Karpstein danced. A new lock, a real lock, a locked lock on the door. No matter, in a mop closet a hole under a sink was covered with drooping canvas—this was Karpstein's private entrance to the room that called to him.

When he entered he saw it was his room. It was his apartment. It was his home from the time when he had a home. His table, his desk, his cloths, his carpet, his vase, his books, his light. Karpstein danced. He danced among his possessions and touched them. He touched the table and then there was no table, no carpet, no desk.

At last the room was almost empty. Only two medium and one small suitcase, bulging all; tied with rope, one cardboard box, a cloth shopping bag and two framed pictures remained in a pile in the middle of the floor. Karpstein danced slowly and without sadness around them.

The *haggadah*, the retelling of the exile. Karpstein did not stop dancing. He knew this tale. In the seventh room on the seventh floor Karpstein saw and played the story of the exile of Karpstein.

First came the workers. A silent circle of ashen palloured familiar faces. Karpstein went and took his place among them. The foreman and the owners were there too. It was the shipping room now in the last factory. Racks and rows of identically garish dresses appeared now in the periphery.

The owners, two brothers named Hass, were speaking. "Circumstances...forced...lost contracts...high costs...not your fault...relocate the factory...margin of profit...loyalty appreciated...one week's pay for each of you."

Gomez, the head of shipping began to cry. He had been there for eighteen years.

"And if you`re ever in South Carolina on vacation or something, please come say hello to us," Sam Hass, the younger brother had actually said.

It was the beginning of the exile.

Karpstein had worked for Hass Dresses for four years. He was fifty-four and looked forty-four. He could work again.

The circle of workers and bosses and dresses was gone. This was the street.

The week's wages was gone. The money from the bank was gone. The small jobs were scarce. The big jobs never came again. The money from selling his desk and his table and most of his books was gone. The apartment was gone.

Only two medium and one small suitcase, bulging all; tied with rope, one cardboard box, a cloth shopping bag and two framed pictures remained. Karpstein danced slowly around them.

As he danced he saw a couch and a bed and a window and empty wine bottles in the space. Karpstein, in his empty theatre of exile in the seventh room on the seventh floor, was in the apartment of Fleischkopf. Fleischkopf was shouting at him. "Get out, get out, get out. Too fucking long. I said OK a couple of days. I can't even get laid around here with you taking up all my space."

Karpstein danced in the street again.

First came the shelter. In the seventh room on the seventh floor Karpstein saw it again. Rows of beds in body stinking rooms. One floor of men waiting for dawn in narrow beds. One floor of women and families—mostly single parents and their crying kids in makeshift cubicles that promised a degree of privacy but gave little. But here on Karpstein's stage was only one room of men. The limit was one week. In the midst of a coughing, snoring, shouting crowd Karpstein fought sleep.

"What am I doing here with the drunk and the drugged and the crazy? If I close my eyes they will kill me."

In the beginning hope danced with fright.

"I will find work again. I have friends who will help me. This is just for a week or two. I will put on my suit and go to an agency."

On the second night the pictures, one a fading print of his parents, the other a picture of himself as a young child, disappeared. On the fourth night one valise, the one with the suit, vanished. On the fifth night one shoe was stolen.

"One fucking shoe, who steals one fucking shoe?"

The shoe was found in a hallway with its lace gone and its thick leather tongue cut out. The tongueless shoe was given a string and taken in by its owner again.

After the shelter was the park. Bushes and trees filled the room on the seventh floor of Karpstein's hideout castle. In their midst Karpstein and seven or ten others shivered on makeshift mattresses of newspapers and rags. Sleep came and went; sometimes chased away by fear and sometimes by cold. Before the sun returned to paint the sky with light, the darkness was shattered by spotlights. A gang of stick-swinging police came raiding and the wakened sleepers ran through brambles to avoid the rain of blows. A cardboard box of personal treasures and trinkets was lost, spread under bushes and trampled into soft earth, during that retreat.

In the seventh room Karpstein relived his exile from its roots. He saw his belongings disappear. A bag left and forgotten, under a bench at a bus stop. A small suitcase bound with string given to a man who held a knife to Karpstein's throat under a bridge.

It never rains under bridges. Cars rumble like thunder, electric trains shoot lightning, dust drizzles down, but it never rains. Karpstein lived under a bridge for a while. Lived, but not slept. The thunder and lightning of bridges, the fear of sharp toothed rats and sharp knifed strangers made sleep stay away from Karpstein. Soon his hands shook and his eyes were red-rimmed like sores. In his building, Karpstein smelled the sourness of unwashed people not sleeping together in cardboard shelters on the damp earth under the bridge.

He closed his eyes and when he opened them he was in a room again. This time it was the synagogue cellar. For six weeks Karpstein slept there and received meals and a small salary in return for sweeping every day, scrubbing the floor on Friday morning and emptying the trash. It was the synagogue where he had marveled at old men in prayer shawls chanting in an unknown tongue; where he had repeated the ritual chant of bar mitzvah. He had at last found some form of sanctuary in that building he had hardly entered in the forty years or more since his ceremony of acceptance into the congregation. Acceptance again, job, a home.

Karpstein danced slowly in a cloud of memory in the empty room on the seventh floor of his warehouse. He remembered his days of return to life. When he wasn't helping in the synagogue Karpstein walked through familiar and unfamiliar streets. Sometimes he imagined that he just stood still and the rows of dreary stores, tenements, playgrounds and people just rolled past him on some huge conveyor belt. He would walk until he could feel his tiredness and then sit, either in a park or in some small coffee shop, and try to understand the echoes of half thoughts and images that droned through his head. He tried to keep a notebook with him to put down—and maybe decipher—the disjunct rush of thoughts. The notebook entries ("A woman kissed the sores of lepers and called them her roses." "If God is not dead, we'll have to kill Him. If my father were not dead I'd have to kill him." "Look for doors." "Broken cup.") turned out to be pages of scrawls that held reality at bay instead of capturing it. In the middle of the tinny reverberations of the life around him—around but not touching him—Karpstein was an island. When he tried to envision his family and friends he saw tombstones. Karpstein was their lone representative in the land of the living but in that land he had difficulty even representing Karpstein.

After a walk Karpstein was in the park. He sat alone on a bench. He was hungry and tried to stir to walk toward home and food. The sun gave a garish edge to everything he saw. The people who walked by appeared like pieces of each other's dreams. The children playing noisily seemed and sounded miles away. The overwhelming sense of unreality frightened Karpstein. He grasped the rough, wooden slats of the bench as if to hold himself to the earth.

Suddenly from the glare of the day and the confusing rush of strangers before him floated a face towards his face. He tried to look away, but a stranger held Karpstein's gaze and would not let go. It was a woman. Her features did not distinguish themselves from others in his vision, but it was a face that demanded he pay attention to it. She stood on the grass some ten yards from him for a long time. Karpstein was confused. It was not someone he recognized, but there was no doubt that her gaze was riveted on him. She moved toward him with movements so slow and small she could have been floating. Her face was open and unreadable. She was perhaps a tired forty years old, but no other description managed to stick beyond the one non-descriptive word, "average". Across the path from him she hesitated and stood silently staring.

She moved forward and spoke to him.

"You look too much like someone I loved. May I kiss you?"

"You may."

She bent from the waist and kissed him awkwardly—aiming for his forehead but touching her lips once, briefly, to the place where forehead met thinning hairline. She backed away and walked slowly up the path, stopping once to turn and gaze at him. She raised her hand in a motionless wave, a frozen salute. Then she was gone and the moment of silence faded back into the commotion that had reigned before.

Karpstein felt sadness near him but not quite touching him. There was a distinct sensation where the woman's lips had touched. It was as if she had marked him there with words he could not see to read. His void was beginning to give way. A stranger had announced to him that he was alive. He got up and began to walk again. For a moment he considered following the direction the woman had taken and trying to find her to ask for another part of her story. No, she was gone.

("…and called them her roses.")

He walked among lengthening shadows through streets he remembered. The woman's mark was still on him.

("…too much like someone I loved.")

It was past the time he usually turned towards his cellar home, darkness had begun to arrive. Among the shadows of his streets the remembered landmarks of his void stood silently. Here he had played. Here, once a vacant lot, now a building, he had buried a pet. Here his family, now all dead or dying, had walked. He approached the side door of the temple; the door that led to his corner of cellar. In the shadows of the synagogue there was movement. Laughter. Two boys—or was it three—worked quickly on the walls of "his" synagogue. Their arms moved like hissing spray cans headed snakes. In their trail were swastikas and venom words. Three—or was it four— shouted in surprise when Karpstein pounced. It had been 20 years since he had trained and tuned his body, but he was still strong. They fell, they fought, they ran.

When they were gone Karpstein wiped at still wet paint with a piece of shirt he had ripped from one of the spray paint snakes. The walls of his synagogue, his home, were bleeding. Red paint blood ran down stone walls. Softly he caressed the wounded walls of the injured sanctuary, dabbing at slashes of wet paint and rubbing away the swastika brands and the bleeding letters spelling "Jew bastards." Gently, but firmly he stroked the walls.

Karpstein hardly heard a car and then another stop behind him on the street. He hardly heard the running feet. When he looked up he was surrounded. He swung, but a baseball bat answered his swing and knocked him off his feet. He rolled and blocked, but there were a dozen or more pairs of feet to hem him in and kick him. A stick splintered on his back. Fists searched for his face. He fought back as he could, but it was almost futile. Through the bursts of pain he felt as though he were watching the fight from some distance.

As consciousness slipped away from him Karpstein's mind and mouth filled with words he had spoken here decades before but long considered forgotten. "*Boruhoo es Adonai hamavoruch. Boruch Adonai hamavoruch l'olom voed.*" It was the chant for the reading of the Torah—the words he had chanted, decades ago in this building he had tried to defend.

✎ *XXXI*

When clocks stop, the Angel of Death walks upon the earth. Blue lights flash in the darkness, but the sounds are grey. Faces say "He is alive." Faces disappear. There are choking tastes and memory smells. The Death Angel is a faceless woman hooded in grey who stalks the dying in hallways of dying.

Above his eyes on unknown ceilings are spiderless spiderwebs. Human voices float around looking for mouths. People in white dance for him. They cannot speak, their lips are painted on their chests. Food is brought, but he has forgotten how to eat. A man kicks giant vegetables through the hallway to frighten unfearing witches.

Pain is bandaged in, tight against the skin. The bandages try to come off in his hands. His hands are tied down. Now the pain is laughing. There is shouting and faces say "He is shouting." His feet are strapped down.

A man with a needle instead of a hand says "This will help you sleep," and pierces him. He is many and they are running. In his sleep the witches come again and spin his bed.

When he awakes his first question is, "Have I lost anything?" When he awakes, the rabbi comes and stares at him. The old man speaks, but some of the words are stolen by birds in the room and the rabbi dances for him.

"A good thing, Karpstein, you did a good thing. A good thing, Karpstein, you did a good thing. A good thing, Karpstein, you did a good thing. A good thing, Karpstein, you did a good thing. A good thing, Karpstein, you did a good thing. A good thing, Karpstein, you did a good thing. A good thing, Karpstein, you did a good thing. A good thing, Karpstein, you did a good thing," the rabbi is singing to him.

"But...sometimes...waiting...foolish...patience...our people...bringing trouble... A good thing, Karpstein, you did a good thing. A good thing, Karpstein, you did a good thing..."

The words are stolen and the rabbi talks faster.
"Sometimes...waiting...foolish...patience...our people...bringing trouble... A good thing, Karpstein, you did a good thing. A good thing, Karpstein, you did a good thing...But a building is only a building and the Torah is the Torah."

Outside there is a long hallway and a frowning nurse walks with keys. The keys jangle and his skin cringes. Doors are locked and the body he sees strapped down may be his.

The serpent becomes a staff again. The Red Sea of his madness is parted and the faceless witches who danced with the faceless Angel of Death are drowned.

In a garden, a woman asks him, "Would you like to go home?"

"I have no home."

"The new rabbi will help you."

Is the old rabbi dead? Did he drown with the Angel of Death? Have the deaths begun? Is the synagogue allowed to stand?

Karpstein, you did a good thing… But a building is only a building and the Torah is the Torah.

In the seventh room of the seventh floor Karpstein sobs alone.
"How did I end up here, like this?" he asks his tears. "Who is left alive? Where are all the others hiding?"
Perhaps only Karpstein was left alive. Perhaps only Karpstein was hiding.

⤙ *XXXII*

He went back. Karpstein went back even though every cell in his brain screamed at him not to go back. He went back to where the woman who swam in oceans of cheap perfume had hovered.

She had liked him. She said she had liked him.

"She liked me."

After dark descending the rust flake covered ladder down 306 biting rungs was a terror. The round air duct was a tower of terror. The dark tunnels below with frightened rats brushing past the shaking legs of frightened man were a terror. But Karpstein needed to see her. Maybe his body longed for her. His body longed for something, maybe it was her. Even more, he longed to talk to her. She was a fragile flower begging for a cigarette, a fuck, a kind word in dark streets. Karpstein remembered where he had seen her and he crawled through his punishing maze to hunt for her.

Cheap whore. A man who shouted loudly for quiet had called her a cheap whore. Whore meant nothing to Karpstein. He had seen whores, he had talked to whores, he had slept with whores. She, he didn't know her name, was different. She was soft and breakable.

On the night he left the hiding room of Mr. Carver, the killer of two men, to run to the room of Mr. Karpstein, the victim of many killers, he had seen the woman who perfumed the street air.

The metal gates in the tunnel squeaked like laughter at the frightened hiding man who risked his hiding to maybe look at, maybe talk to a brittle looking hooker who might not even be there.

Eighty-seven groping steps through a sour smelling cavern, hundreds of steps, he panicked and lost count, through the underground passageway to his private vestibule and the metal ladder to the heavy iron disk that was his doorway in the street.

Moon and streetlight made his shadow dance on walls, sometimes in front, sometimes in back of him. Karpstein tried to hide in his own shadow.

He didn't bring his food collecting sack with him. There was food in the hidden room. His craving was for a breath of perfume to carry back to his cell.

Karpstein walked in fear along deserted night streets. He ran his crouching, scuttle-run through garbage-paved alleys. He hid from other nighttime wanderers and found an open doorway to melt into when a police car crawled by slowly. He knew where he had seen her; where she had seen him and talked to him. But he didn't know where he would find her again.

Dim, brick wall building; window above door above empty store above street. Window where man yelled for quiet now dark and closed. The perfume was gone. The woman was not there.

She had asked him for a cigarette so many months ago when he had seen her. Now he had found a cigarette—two cigarettes in a lost pack in an alley. He saved them as a gift offering for the perfumed street woman who now was not there.

Karpstein, trying to be just another shadow, walked the shadow-rich streets and hid in the darkened crevices of the night. If he had known her name he would have whispered it into the obscure corners.

On a street not far from where he had seen her he saw a woman. His heart quickened its rhythms. Suddenly he wanted to run, to return to his solitary nest. What would he say to this woman who might not remember she had once said she liked him? Would she still like him?

The woman stood at the curb and looked intently one way and then the other as if she were looking for a taxi. A car cruised by. Karpstein hid, but from his silhouetted cranny he could see her step forward, almost into the street, and strike a pose that seemed a caricature of whore, of Magdalene, of streetwalking slut from every age. With pelvis thrust forward and thigh extended she watched the car intently and then, when it passed without slowing, fell back to her more careless stance and jabbed her middle finger at the air in the direction the car had gone.

Karpstein walked timidly in her direction. She turned toward him, ready to open again into her business pose. When she saw him she dropped back a step and turned back toward the street as if he had never been there. The streetlight shone on her face. It was not the woman he remembered. It was not the perfume-exuding whore who had approached him as he escaped home one evening through these same silent avenues. But he would ask her about the other one. He was not sure what he would ask, but he would ask. He would describe. He would inquire about someone he had never really met, but someone he longed to see again, to talk to.

Karpstein paused and started to stammer his strange query.

"Get lost, creep!"

The woman's voice spat past him like a snarl. It simmered with contempt. Where the woman he sought had been fragile and even gentle, this one was hard and hateful.

"Get lost," she repeated. "I don't do it for free and I don't do it with bums. Go in the alley and fuck your hand if you're horny, you fucking creep."

He stared at her. Her face was a mask of malice. It was not hatred in general, but loathing for him personally and specifically that glowed from her harsh features. He stood transfixed for a moment by the scalding shaft of emotional acid being directed at him. She clawed open her purse and pulled forth a knife.

"I ain't kidding, fuckface. Get the hell out of here."

A trembling Karpstein was gone in an instant.

Karpstein ran. Karpstein ran where not even the glint of streetlight on knifeblade would find him. In an instant the whores came out. Wherever Karpstein ran through the night streets, the whores were there too, beckoning to him, reaching out to him, calling to him, but not one of them was the whore whose company he sought.

"Hey, baby baby baby," a fat whore called him "baby."

"Do you want it? Do you want it?" lisped a tall, black, male whore whose false eyelashes were heavy with gold glitter.

"Don't run away, honey," pleaded a trembling whore with a swollen shut, black eye.

Out of doorways and windows, out of alleyways and alcoves, out of every niche and nook it seemed to him that hands were reaching out to try to grasp him as he ran.

Then he found her. In an alleyway of darkness and bad smells he found her. He found her by her sound and not by sight. She was leaning over a garbage can and throwing up when he found her. He peered into the darkness. Yes, it was she. The perfume he remembered as much as he remembered her face did not reach him. A wall of other odors stood between them.

She stood up, spitting out ugly tastes, gasping and coughing. She dabbed at her mouth with a wadded paper tissue.

She looked at him.

"Are you OK?

"No, I ain't OK. I'm sick. Fucking greasy hamburger made me sick."

She hiccuped. Karpstein was afraid she would throw up again. People vomiting always made him feel sick too, but he decided he wouldn't run away from her even if she heaved again.

"What's it to you how I feel? You the fucking county health commissioner or something?"

Her belligerent tone was a mask. Karpstein was frightened by the hostile behavior, but he stayed.

"I just asked."

She stared at him without any sign of recognition, but she softened slightly.

"Who are you?"

"I—I—I met you before."

"Where?"

"Near here."

"Did you fuck me?"

"No, I ran away."

She stared at him. The streetlight cast a dim glow into the alley. She remembered him.

"You."

"You asked me for a cigarette. Here, I brought you some."

She looked at him as if she were trying to see something inches beneath his skin. She took the took the pack and pulled out one of the cigarettes. She never took her eyes off him.

"Thanks. This will help. My mouth tastes like day old cat piss."

She lit the butt and took a deep drag.

"You wanna go upstairs to my room?"

"I don't have any money."

"You didn't have money that time either. Why did you run away from me? I was dying to talk to somebody."

"Afraid."

"Of me?"

"Getting caught."

"Afraid your wife will catch you?"

"I have no wife. I am alone. I am hiding."

"So why did you come back now?"

"Now I am dying to talk to somebody. You said you liked me."

She laughed. "Yeah, I like you. Sometimes I like everybody. What are you hiding from?"

"The patrols."

"Hey you ain't some kind of escaped nut or a killer or something...?"

"No, I am a Jew."

"That's OK by me. I'm about half Jewish. My old man was a Jew...or at least his mother was. I don't know what that makes me."

"Aren't you afraid?"

"Afraid? Fuck, honey, I ain't afraid of nothing. I carry a switchblade and I can run like fucking hell if I have to."

She paused and took another deep drag.

"Hey, thanks for the cig. You want the other one?"

"No, I don't smoke."

"And you brought these just for me?" She began looking deep into him again.

"I found them. I remembered you asked for one."

"You remembered me?" she asked with a puzzled shake of her head.

"...and your perfume."

She just shook her head again.

"I call myself Babs. What about you?"

"Karpstein."

"That's it, just Karpstein? No first name."

He thought for a few seconds.

"You can call me Tiboreleh."

"Tiboreleh?? What the hell kind of name is that?"

"I think its Hungarian. My grandparents used to call me that. My grandmother was from Hungary."

"I'll just call you Karpstein, if you don't mind."

"I don't mind, Babs."

She took his hand.

"Let's go up to my room. We can sit and talk there. I don't feel like working tonight anyway. I don't feel so good. I'll make it up tomorrow with all the guys from the factory district who want a blowjob during lunch hour."

Babs' room like Carver's room was like Karpstein's room. Upstairs in a rotting building lived a person who was not hiding but whose small room was like a hiding nest. In Babs' room there was a sad attempt to be erotic, to be seductive, to be inviting. Failed. In Babs' room there were curtains on the wall around the bed. There were *Kama Sutra* pictures of Indian gods screwing each other into nirvana thumbtacked to cracking paint. There was a lamp with two bulbs of which one was red to lend a redlight mood to a sad room with a sagging bed where fucking was a business.

"This is my son," she said about a poorly framed picture of a blond toddler.

"You have a son," said Karpstein who had no son.

"I have a son."

"Do you still feel sick," said Karpstein, the father who had no children, in a lurch of non sequitur.

"No, I'm OK now," said Babs who never really knew a father.

She looked at Karpstein. She was constantly on watch for a sign of his true motivation for being kind.

"Where do you live?"

"I don't live, I hide."

"Where do you hide?"

"In a place in this part of the city. Please don't ask."

"What is your life?"

"Hiding."

"Why?"

Suddenly Karpstein, who knew why he was hiding, who knew who were his enemies, who knew the danger, who knew the answers, could not answer. Karpstein whose pain was the pain of memories, felt no pain, but started to cry. At first, only unwelcome, boiling tears burned his eyes and rolled down his cheeks. Then, when the tears had dissolved him, the sobs began to crack his walls.

"Why?"

She had asked him why. Now he was crying and sobbing and his head was cradled on the Babs' lap. She held his shoulders and stroked him. She rocked him gently. Why was he hiding; she asked him why.

Softly, in silence, they held each other. Alone, in despair, they comforted each other.

The woman spoke. "Do you want to fuck me?"

Karpstein trembled. He looked up at her with fright in his eyes.

"Do you want to make love to me?" Babs asked him.

More tears rolled down his face. After a pause he nodded slowly.

Karpstein clung to her. They clung to each other, naked and wanting. Karpstein caressed the woman gently and her tears began to leave their hiding places to flow in open air.

"Please stay with me tonight," she asked him after their flesh and their juices had mingled and their passion had come back to a more level place. "Nobody ever stays with me. Nobody ever touches me gently and holds me. I don't want to wake up alone tomorrow. Please stay with me until morning."

"I can only go home in the dark—after the people are gone from the streets. I can only go home when they can't see me."

"You can hide here until dark again. I have some money, I can feed you."

∾ *XXXIII*

A dog followed Karpstein home. It didn't follow him all the way home
because no creature without opposing thumbs could climb the final,
rusty ladder into the murky skybox that Karpstein called his home. The
dog came to him in a street near the place where the whores gathered.
It came to him as a person might to ask for directions or a match or
alms. It came directly to him even though there were other people to be
seen on those dark streets. It was a brown dog, perhaps black, maybe
grey. It was an ordinary dog; a not easy to remember dog—except for
its eyes. The dog came to him as if to ask him something and looked
into him, through him with eyes as deep as wells. The dog didn't speak

to him, but Karpstein heard the questions it would have asked. Karpstein was not fearful of the dog who knew hunter from hunted.

He reached a hand toward the dog and the dog who was not fearful of the hunted came to him and licked the hand. When he went on, the dog followed him or walked with him or even walked ahead on the path Karpstein had chosen. When Karpstein hid in dark shadows the dog, silent as a shadow hid beside him.

When they arrived in the final courtyard, where the heavy manhole cover opened like a door into hell to lead Karpstein to his paradise, they sat in a dark corner and waited.

"Who are you dog? Who sent you to follow me?"

The dog looked at him as if trying to understand the words and formulate an answer.

"It is said that the great prophet and teacher, Elijah takes all shapes. Shall I bless you by saying blessed teacher—*Boruch aboh, rebbe?*"

The dog looked silently at Karpstein. It leaned its head close to his face and sniffed his mouth. Its eyes took every glimmer of the fading light and made green, glowing coals. The effect was supernatural and even though Karpstein had seen animals' eyes phosphorescent in the semi-darkness before, he shuddered as the dog looked into him and through him again.

"*Boruch aboh, rebbe,*" he muttered again. "Are you here to test me? Must I give you food now to prove that I am a man of *tzedukah*—of charity?"

Karpstein offered forth a small bag containing a loaf of fresh bread and some cheese sandwiches that Babs had given him when he left. The glowing eyed dog sniffed and turned away.

"Is my offering refused, rebbe? Am I damned then?"

The dog turned back and looked at him and then licked his hand. Karpstein reached into the bag and tore off a chunk of bread. He held it forward toward the dog who crouched at his feet.

"Eat, rebbe."

This time the dog did not turn away. It eyed the bread and sniffed and, using one paw to hold it down, chewed off pieces until there was none left. When the dog had finished eating, Karpstein struggled to standing.

"Now, rebbe, it's dark enough and I can climb up to my tower. Goodbye, rebbe. I hope we meet again in this life."

The dog wagged its tail gently and watched while Karpstein went to the manhole cover, checked to see that his sliver of wood was undisturbed, that no one else had used the entrance since he left, and then struggled to move the heavy metal disk. The dog stood watch while Karpstein climbed down into the darkness and pulled the cover closed behind himself. Then the dog came and sniffed the covered hole where his new friend had disappeared, peed on it and withdrew, glowing eyes and all, into the shadows.

XXXIV

In his room alone Karpstein imagined a river; watched his river; listened to his river. He felt and saw the cold warm murky clear quiet roaring river where monsters hid and thought fish swam too fast to touch.

River of exile flowed into itself. Beginningless river, endless river. Karpstein's never existing river was always there. Karpstein swam in his forever river, deep in its shadows, floating slowly in its rushing currents; racing through its still pools.

Karpstein drowned in the river of exile. His body, like a bloated doll with helpless arms and gaping jaw, eyes open—not seeing-was carried through the rooms and echoes of his exile. Carried, then cast up dry to breathe again and remember the river.

Karpstein lived in his exile. His exile was his home. He inhaled his exile, wore his exile and submerged himself in it.

"I will go home," he thought and the only home he had was called exile.

"Where are the living?" he asked, and the dead tried to answer him. The difference was hard to know.

Carver is living—and the woman of the street is living. His father is dead. Yet he spoke to them all. He saw them. He used the same language, the same grammar, the same syntax to speak to them all. And after he spoke to them they were all gone.

The rats at the secret entrance of his tower were living. Tonight, as he returned from his night prowl with a burlap bag of scavenged food, a rat, a very much living rat had run helter skelter towards him. The real rat, merging with nightmare-provoking image of rats, had leaped onto Karpstein's leg for a brief moment before squealing blindly off to a hiding place.

"Maaaaaa," was Karpstein's shrill and self-surprising scream of terror as he and frightened rat each fled for shelter. In primal fear he shreiked for the mother who feared and hated rats as much as he did; for the mother who no longer existed; for the mother he had abandoned and the mother who had always abandoned him.

His trembling cry rang out in empty space, mocking him with its reverberations. The walls around him called out for his mother who might never come again.

Karpstein was shaking and sweating as he pulled the creaking, metal door of the round chamber closed behind him.

He put down his food sack and slumped on the floor against the round, metal wall. He was breathing hard. A short rest and then he would go on. He was safe there. The rats never came there.

In the darkness the chamber had transformed for Karpstein. He was once again in the cellar of the building where he lived before Big Al died.

"Don't play down in the basement. You'll get hurt down there," his mother yelled at him.

But he always went there. In the smelly, dark rooms and damp corners he could hide alone and think his thoughts. He could play his games of make-believe and magic without being stared at or questioned or sent on idle errands or yelled at.

Karpstein's cellar was a city. Basements of three buildings joined together by broken-lock doors formed a suite of dark spaces where knights could kill dragons, soldiers sneak up on the enemy and explorers could force open the doors of curse-ridden tombs to discover lost civilizations.

Once, at the end of his three basements, Karpstein found a sealed doorway where a fourth building had once been part of the chain. Loose boards provided an entrance for the young explorer.

Karpstein pried the boards aside and crawled into the new territory. Like the bear who went over the mountain only to find nothing more than the other side of the mountain, Karpstein found the new region disappointingly similar to the one he had just left.

There, there were rooms; here, there were rooms. There, there were assorted treasures—the left-over junk of generations of tenants. Here, the treasures inventoried differently, but even to the eyes of a nine-year-old, they were pretty much the same.

Someone lived in young Karpstein's newly conquered cellar. There was a mattress and a scattering of belongings in one tiny room. He sat on the mattress and viewed the chamber with awe. The thought that people could live in something other than an apartment with kitchen and living room and bathroom had not really entered his consciousness before.

Later that night he dreamed he had left his parents and lived alone in such a room. In his dream the darkness overwhelmed him and he woke up crying and calling for his mother. Awake and sobbing, he called again and again. She didn't come—no one came.

After a half-dozen cries, a distant voice, gravely with sleep, responded, "Teddy, go to sleep."

Now, in his cellar of fright there were only echoes. No voice came from another room urging him to sleep. The shadows around him stopped moving. Karpstein pulled himself to his feet, tied his food sack to his waist and began the long ascent up the rough ladder that would take him to his hidden sky cave.

He was still shaking from his encounter with the rat and his encounter with his childhood dream. His legs felt weak. An ice wind blew inside him. Several time he thought he was falling. His trembling hands were holding hurting tight to biting rungs. His body was pressed hard against the ladder. He was not falling; was not even slipping, but the pervasive wind of fright out-wailed the calmer breeze of safe reality.

Karpstein struggled to the top with his needed cargo of food. He struggled past the top and through his air-duct entrance, lowered himself to the floor and was home.

He had craved peaceful rest, but he'd no chance to close his eyes. Karpstein had a visitor. This was not the first time he had seen this man in his building. Before it had always been a distant glance. This time it was in the sanctuary.

The visitor was thin—too thin. His face bones seemed covered with pale cloth instead of skin. His chin and nose were uncommonly pointed. He wore black, threadbare trousers and a tattered black coat with tails. The strange figure was hatless, but it wouldn't have been surprising to see him wearing a tall, black hat. Karpstein stared at the stranger, but the other seemed not to notice he was being observed.

After a while Karpstein fell asleep. When he woke up the visitor was gone.

∞ *XXXV*

Fireflies danced in the grass of the park. Fireflies rose up, blinked, flew and blinked again. Karpstein saw fireflies blinking in the half dark of summer nights and knew they were magic. Teddy Karpstein caught fireflies and put them in glass jars to keep their light forever with him. But magic is never forever and dead fireflies in jars were just dead bugs. Sad, dried up creatures sharing the darkness with a young boy who wanted to believe in magic.

It was during the blustery prelude to winter when fireflies came in to Karpstein's hiding place. Karpstein was not there to watch the fireflies dance when they first came in, but soon he would see the magic they made. It was cold that night. Cold and alone the watchman who night after night guarded the portals of Karpstein's tower stared into the glowing coil of an electric heater. The heater glared up at him from the floor near his feet. It warmed a zone just large enough to make it possible for one part of a body to be too hot and another to still be chilled.

The lonely watchman had come to know that his life and this vigil were intertwined. There were no other jobs he could find. The idea of reading or studying while the night crawled past him had long since been abandoned. He was here and here was where he was. He tipped a bottle of whiskey to his lips in an attempt to bring the abundant warmth enjoyed by his legs up to his throat and chest as well. The attempt didn't succeed, but the whiskey numbness made him forget the cold.

He tried not to think of Karpstein who lived in a hidden space over his head. He did not succeed. Karpstein was part of his mental landscape. Karpstein was his neighbor and a warning to his future. Karpstein was his prisoner and he was Karpstein's prisoner. Together they spent the nights in silence in a dreary building dedicated to remnants of the past. Just ten floors and not much more separated them, the tired watchman often thought.

The watchman slept.

In the alley a nameless man almost slept. He was too cold to sleep. He was too cold to live. Some morning; any morning he might be a nameless winter corpse in the freezer drawers of the city. His toe tag would say "unknown" and his obituary, if there was room for one between the advertisements and the wars, would say "unidentified, homeless man dies in alley."

But this night he would not freeze. This night he would seek warmth and find warmth.

Filth encrusted clothing crackled as the freezing man prowled closer to the door with the light and the warmth. The door, unlocked, moaned gently on its hinges. The sleeping watchman stirred but didn't waken. The freezing man felt warmth. He kept crawling, pulling his aching body along the hallway past the watchman's door. The same path had been used by Karpstein many times during his exile. The crawling man smelled whiskey from the sleeping watchman and he longed for some, but his need to find a warm place took precedence. The sleeping watchman did not smell the embedded fetor from the clothing of the crawling man.

The man found a door and pushed against it. It opened onto a stairway. Down a small flight of stairs there was a pile of old cardboard boxes and other trash. The homeless man had found a home—at least for one cold night. Now there were three souls sheltered in the building that protected Karpstein and his memories.

The visitor flattened several layers of cardboard as a mattress and laid down. It was still cold, but not as death inviting as the outdoor cold.

The man shivered instead of sleeping. The cold in his bones would not go away. He got up and gathered some torn pieces of cardboard and paper. He pushed them into a pile in a corner of the concrete and metal stair landing. He fumbled in his pocket and found a crushed book of matches. The first three matches died at birth. The fourth was accepted by an edge of paper and a weak flame fluttered into a full dance of smoke and fire.

Warmth. The man hovered over his fire child and nourished it with pieces of paper and packing material. Warmth at last.

Fireflies danced in the park of Karpstein's childhood. Fireflies danced in Karpstein's head. Fireflies danced in the building where Karpstein, wrapped in ragged blankets, slept; where the watchman, wrapped in alcohol, slept and where the homeless man, wrapped in the warmth of his fire, finally fell asleep.

Fireflies swirled on paths of smoke to dance in a pile of trash. Fireflies found wooden walls to play on. Fireflies raced for the ceiling. Fireflies multiplied as fire rose higher and reached for food.

The man who had invited the fireflies to dance on the stairway awoke. A grinning red mouth grew bigger on his jacket. He watched the mouth for a long moment and then tore the jacket off and threw it into the flaming corner. He opened the door and ran through the corridor past the sleeping watchman and out to the cold alley. He ran to the freezing nighttime street and kept running; running as if the flames he had started were chasing him. He ran blindly and clumsily. He ran until his heart stopped and he fell dead.

Thick tentacles of smoke accompanied by the sound of roaring flames thrashed through the hallway and woke the watchman. He ran to the door of his room and looked toward the sound. The flickering orange glow of fire danced on every wall.

"Fire," he gasped and ran to the telephone. "Fire."

Fire danced on the walls and floors. Fire found dancing partners in the myriad debris heaps accumulated in nooks and niches everywhere. Firefly sparks whirlpooled like crowns of stars around the heads of gyrating fire demons. The fire laughed with the crackling, deep throated roar that is the voice of fire.

The frightened watchman saw the walls welcome the fire and he thought of Karpstein hiding far above him. In cinema he would have been a hero. In another life he would have disregarded his own safety and raced to save the strange Jew who hid in the building he was paid to guard. But this was not another life and far from cinema. This was a smoke-filled, throat-burning hell of real life and Karpstein was so far away.

Screaming firetrucks filled the streets around the ghost-crowded mansion where Karpstein lived. The watchman ran out to meet the first ones on the scene.

"A man. Hiding. Hiding in the attic." He gestured frantically. "Up there. Up there. His name is Karpstein."

The firemen attacked the fire demons like soldiers. Hoses gushed and spewed and flaming piles of garbage dissolved in sputtering streams.

A rescue team, following the instructions of an hysterical watchman, raced for the stairs to take the aerobic dash to find a man named Karpstein who might or not be hiding so high above them.

The curling eddies of smoke swooshed ahead of them. The towerlike tube through which Karpstein entered his hidden chamber carried the smoke clouds and the fire demon voice up to him. He struggled to breathe as he untied the ladder and opened his trapdoor. When the hatchway opened, a burst of clear air greeted him. He leaned hard against the ladder and it creaked its way down. He descended. The hallway was cool and quiet. No smoke stung him here. He ran toward the dim red light and pulled open the door. There was no smoke yet in the stairway. He knew there was a fire somewhere below him and he knew it was time to leave his place of hiding.

Karpstein started down the stairs. Then, from many floors below, he heard the sound he had been waiting years to hear.

Heavily booted feet ran toward him. Distant voices echoed up the stairwell. Boots. A patrol. Boots thudded in the direction of his secret place. He was found. The smoke was a trick to make him reveal his clandestine nest.

A claw of pain took hold of Karpstein's chest. Who had turned him in? Who had known his secret world and sent the boots to find him?

He ran for his ladder. He would not be taken easily. They would need to do more than merely outstretch their arms to round up this Jew. His fear painted full-blown pictures of the boot steps pounding up ever nearer to him. He saw the stormtroopers coming closer to drag him away.

Noxious clouds scratched at Karpstein's eyes and throat as he returned to his lair. The howling roar of fire filled him with terror. The smoke snakes surrounded him. He dragged his red chair under the skylight and climbed up.

Through the skylight the night shone star-filled. He pulled himself up to the roof. The air was crisp and the cool air invigorated him. A sense of safety possessed him. A thin wisp of smoke curled through a vent, but it carried no sensation of threat. Here there was peace. Here Karpstein was alone.

Below, the gushing hoses slapped back the demons of flame. Axes chewed away smoldering wallboards and rooted out the fireflies that threatened to eat the building. Steam hissed the defeat song of the dying fire serpents.

The rescue squad pulled open the stairway door beneath Karpstein's drab penthouse.

"Karpstein, Karpstein, where are you?"

Flashlights pierced the darkness. The firemen did not know why a man was hiding here in a burning storage place, but the watchman said he was there and their job was rescue.

Booted feet climbed Karpstein's ladder.

"Karpstein, Karpstein, where are you?"

On the roof, Karpstein heard them coming for him. He knew they would come. He knew in his heart that the crushing boots would reverberate in his hiding place. So many hidden ones had been found and dragged away. Now they had found him. Karpstein's hiding was over.

"Karpstein, Karpstein, where are you?"

Karpstein was afraid. Do bullets hurt, he wondered. Would they beat him? Perhaps they would just shoot him. Do bullets hurt?

"Karpstein, Karpstein, where are you?"

"Karpstein, Karpstein, where are you?"

"Karpstein, Karpstein, where are you?"

Karpstein was hiding. The men with boots had found him. Now they would torture him and drag him to the camps. Would they beat him? Perhaps they would just shoot him. Do bullets hurt? Do bullets hurt?

Airshaft. Karpstein stepped to the edge of the airshaft. There below in the land of fallen belongings, of lost things, was safety. It was silent there. It was peaceful there and silent. Among the forsaken mattresses and abandoned tables Karpstein could rest. There were no booted men looking for him there. There was no roar of fire and no serpents of smoke in the dark airshaft.

Karpstein was tired. In his heart there was tranquility. The serene darkness summoned him. Behind him he heard the boots and the voices.

"Karpstein, Karpstein, where are you?"

"Karpstein, Karpstein, where are you?"

Karpstein stepped to the edge of the roof.

"I must find a new place to hide," he thought.

And he stepped off into the darkness.

About the Author

Martin A. David has published a wide variety of non-fiction including *The Dancer's Audition Book* (Sterling Publ; NY, London) and hundreds of articles for publications such as the *Los Angeles Times*. His short stories and poetry have appeared in magazines and been published electronically. *Karpstein Was Hiding* is his first published novel.

In addition to writing, he has been a professional actor, modern dancer and choreographer, mime and clown.

In the late 1980s he returned to school and became a computer software engineer and technical writer.

He is a translator whose published translations of books by classical Danish authors have received acclaim in Europe. He is fluent in Danish, Spanish and French and has conversational grasp of three or four other languages. He is a member of the American Translators Association.

Martin was born in Brooklyn, New York and grew up in Staten Island. From 1966 to 1976 he lived in Paris, Rome and Copenhagen. He currently resides in California with his wife, Sarah.